DEATH BY DENIAL

Peter Black, an accomplished physician, calls upon these skills as his hero Dr Duncan "Mac" MacGregor finds his first-hand knowledge of Covid needs to be heard. Instead, he finds himself on another adventure filled journey with plot twists and obstacles until the book's conclusion.

– Amazon review

Awesome book and great read!

– Amazon review

BERSERKER

Fiction by Peter Black

Seizure

Death by Denial

Berserker

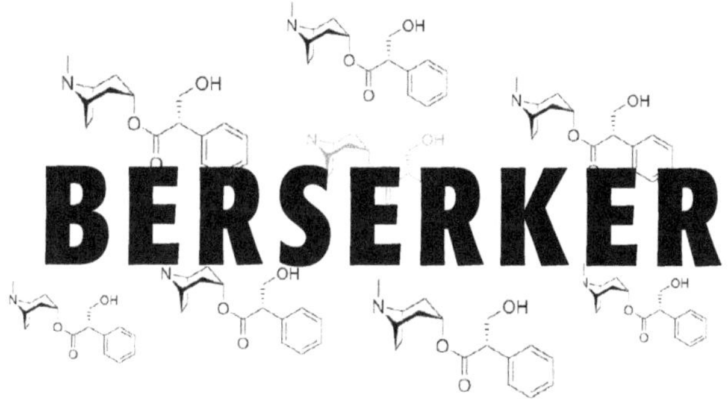

BERSERKER

A DUNCAN MACGREGOR NOVEL

PETER BLACK

Skean Dhu Press
Cambridge, Massachusetts

Skean Dhu Press
Cambridge, MA
Skeandhupress.com

Publisher's Note: This is a work of fiction. Names, characters, places, and incidents are a product of the author's imagination. Locales and public names are sometimes used for atmospheric purposes. Any resemblance to actual people, living or dead, or to businesses, companies, events, institutions, or locales is completely coincidental.

Cover and text design by Mayapriya Long, Bookwrights
Printed in the United States of America

Berserkers/PeterBlack.—1st ed.

ISBN 978-1-952683-07-7, paperback
ISBN 978-1-952683-08-4, hardbound
ISBN 978-1-952683-06-0, ebook
ISBN 978-1-952683-09-1, audio book

This novel is dedicated to all who face and fight
domestic terrorism in America

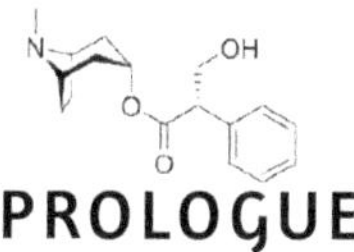

PROLOGUE

THE NOVICE AND THE POWDER

Fourteen-year-old Uhtric felt his heart hammer in his chest. He ducked once more behind the rock hiding him from the sea.

On the beach in front of him, dozens of warriors descended from ships shallow enough to land directly on his beloved Lindisfarne shore. The narrow vessels with prows carved to resemble snakes frightened him.

The invaders frightened him even more. Giants with golden hair, long beards, and thick wool tunics, a few wore iron helmets and chain mail vests. Each carried a circular shield as well as ax, spear, or sword.

They clustered on the beach close enough for him to smell their sweat. Their language was barbaric, so different from the smooth Latin he heard at Mass each day. He looked up the hill at the mud flats between him and the priory. *No way to make it back to safety without being seen.*

His brief sojourn to the beach had turned into a nightmare. Terror engulfed the Lindisfarne novice. *Who were these men, and what would they do to the people he loved?*

Despite the cool day, perspiration beaded on Uhtric's brow. As he stared at the gathering, eight men wearing bearskins over their heads separated from the group and formed a circle. A hooded figure moved to the center of the group and began to chant.

Uhtric realized with a jolt it was a woman. She had to be a priestess. Uhtric knew religious rituals, but he had never seen a ceremony like this, so different from the daily mass he participated in as a novice at the priory.

The bearskin warriors passed a flask around, pouring liquid into small cups that each one held. The woman took a pouch from her belt and poured powder into each cup. Each man swallowed his potion in one gulp.

After a few minutes, the eight men paced and muttered and began to pound their spears against the sand. Their teeth chattered and they started to shiver, sweating and howling like animals. One man bit into the top of his wooden shield, screamed, and ran toward Uhtric's hiding place.

Uhtric froze, eyes wide, breath coming in gasps. *The warrior had discovered him.*

As the invader drew closer, Uhtric could see bulging eyeballs and fluid dripping from eye sockets and nose. He closed his eyes and waited for a fatal blow from the invader's sword.

It never came. Instead, he heard a body hit the ground. Looking around his outcrop, he saw the warrior lying motionless on the ground.

The priestess moved to the body, bent over to hold a metal mirror in front of the man's mouth, seemed satisfied that she saw no breath on the mirror, and walked away.

The violent warrior had become a corpse. *What mysterious force had killed him?*

The remaining potion drinkers charged up the hill toward the church, howling, slashing at dogs, trees, everything in their path. They did not seem bothered by the sudden death of their comrade, or by anything else.

Uhtric realized he would be killed if he could not protect himself. He crawled to the dead warrior, poked the corpse to be sure there was no response, and slid the man's blade from its sheath. He recognized the weapon as a seax, about a forearm's length, razor sharp at the tip.

His appreciation for the weapon was interrupted by the unmistakable scream of the priestess running toward him with a dagger in her uplifted right hand.

He had no time to think. Still lying on his back, he grabbed the seax, thrust it in front of his body with both hands, and turned his head, anticipating his own bloody death.

The woman's right arm brushed by his ear, embedding her knife in the ground as her torso impaled itself on his blade. Eyes blazing inches from his face, she shouted a few words in her obscene language. Her breath was foul, and bloody phlegm issued forth from her mouth. In seconds, her twisting stopped, her eyes glazed and became fixed. She lay limp against his body, her robe covering him with its strange incense smell.

Uhtric left the blade transfixing her, crawled out from under the corpse, and raced away from this inconceivable scene with pounding heart and twisting stomach.

He slowed down as he approached the priory and hid behind an upturned wagon.

The warriors he had seen on the beach prowled this way and that, thrusting swords at anything that moved. They seemed to be in a trance, oblivious to everything around them. Townsmen, women, children, monks lay in widening pools of blood, skulls split by axes or torsos transfixed. A crazed bear-skin wearer stabbed one of his own kind in the back, bellowing like a bull while his countryman bled to death.

As Uhtric watched, marauders poured out of the doors of St. Cuthbert's chapel. Some drove priests in chains before them. Others carried sacks stuffed with sacred objects used in the daily celebration of the Mass—golden orbs, silver chalices, bronze candlesticks.

He waited for the invaders to pass and crept into the priory. Blood collected in pools around the corpses of his former teachers and friends. Heads lay separated from bodies.

Uhtric bent over and vomited. He could not block out the stench of blood and stool and sweat. The pagans appeared to have taken everything—all the treasures of the monastery.

St. Cuthbert! Had they violated the most precious possession of the priory, the relics and body of its patron saint? He rushed to the wooden casket inconspicuously placed behind the altar and ripped off its plain woolen shroud.

The casket was untouched. Uhtric embraced it as if it were a lost friend, sobbing at the agony of all he had witnessed, and passed out.

He woke as shadows lengthened in the waning sun.

Staggering to a window, unable to experience any further emotion, Uhtric saw a cluster of the invaders form a circle around a freshly dug grave preparing to bury the priestess. One of the warriors removed the pouch from the priestess's belt and held it up to the sky. With his other hand he raised a hollow golden orb stolen from the priory's treasury. The invaders chanted as the warrior ceremoniously poured the powder from the priestess's pouch into the orb, sealed it, and placed it in the pocket of the corpse's robe.

The invaders lowered the body into the ground with ropes, then shoveled dirt and stone over it to create a mound.

The tide was high, but about to change. The men marched to the shore, boarded their ships, and left as quickly as they had come.

Uhtric wept. In less than eight hours, these marauders had destroyed everything he loved. He picked up a page of vellum from the priory floor and scratched the scene—ships, warriors, priestess, priory, orb. To underscore the importance of the orb, he drew rays of light emanating from it. The powder in that small orb had released savagery beyond measure.

Uhtric never forgot the brutality and devastation of that attack. He joined the Lindisfarne monastery as a scribe and kept his sketch as a bookmark for his bible. Each day he meditated on his sketch as a sign of the unpredictability of earthly life.

Over the years, Uhtric learned more about the violent warriors of the Northmen called Berserkers. Universally feared in their animal skins, they formed the first line of attack in Norse raids on England and Europe. These were the men who had drunk the powder. After he learned to write, he scratched on the vellum the danger of what he called Berserker powder, a drug that could turn men into wild animals.

On his deathbed, Uhtric sewed his precious vellum sheets between the leaves of the back cover of his bible. He clutched the bible to his chest as he passed gently from this life to the next.

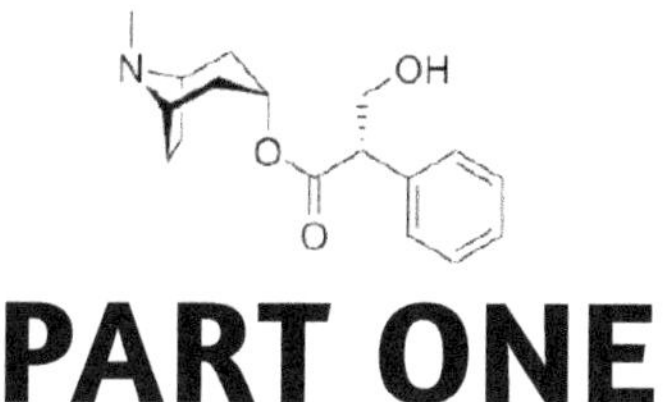

PART ONE

BERSERKER POWDER RETURNS

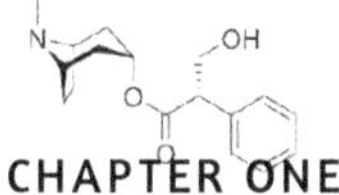

CHAPTER ONE

CORPSES

TANGIER, MOROCCO
JANUARY 21, 2021

D r. Duncan MacGregor scanned the corpses with the practiced eye of a neurosurgeon. His CIA colleague, Jim Brogan, had asked him to investigate these deaths, and he felt at ease in the morgue of Tangier's Hassan V Hospital.

The middle-aged male victim on the autopsy table had chunks of hair and scalp ripped away, right eye torn out of its socket, half of the right ear bitten off. A dead macaque hung by its jaws from the victim's neck. The monkey's body covered the man's chest, clenched fangs embedded in neck muscles and carotid artery.

"We don't need your help for this case, Dr. MacGregor," the policeman standing beside Mac said. His elegant French accent did not hide his antagonistic tone. "Spend your time in Tangier sightseeing. We'll take care of the investigation."

"Do you have any idea what we might be dealing with, Duroc?" Mac asked.

"Of course not," the policeman replied. "And please address me as Prefect Duroc. We are just starting our analysis, but we have our procedures, and an American neurosurgeon has no place in them."

"Have you heard of Ebola?" Mac asked. "This monkey

could be carrying the next pandemic. Why did it attack this man? And why did the monkey die in the process?"

Mac turned toward the police chief to emphasize his point, wincing at the stale cigarette breath that met him. "My job is to understand why a typically docile macaque ambushed and killed a man ten times its size. Your assignment, as I understand it, is to assist me."

The prefect straightened to his full height. "You are correct, but we have no resources to help you right now. We cannot perform a postmortem until our pathologist returns from vacation."

"Is there no one else to examine the corpses?"

"Not in Tangier."

"What about Rabat or Casablanca?"

"Tangier police take care of Tangier problems."

"Then I will do the autopsies myself," Mac said.

"But that is impossible."

"The King has given me medical privileges while I'm here, and you have been given your orders to help me." He scanned the room and added, "I'll need protective equipment."

"It is not my job to provide."

"Find someone whose job it is."

"I have an associate who may help," Duroc said, then shouted, "Amara, *viens ici*!"

A woman in her twenties with jet-black hair, bright eyes, and light brown skin entered the autopsy room. She wore a similar police uniform to Duroc's—dark jacket and pants, white shirt, and tie. Duroc's uniform was wrinkled and ill-fitting. Hers was a fashion statement. "Officer Amara Zadi, this is Dr. Duncan MacGregor from Boston," Duroc said. "Give him what help you can spare. I must attend to other matters." Duroc exited with an air of great self-importance.

"Doctor MacGregor, I am glad to see a Bostonian here in Tangier," the woman said in perfect English. "I did post-graduate work at Boston University. I anticipated that you might want to do an autopsy, so I gathered some items you might need."

She stepped aside to reveal a full cart of personal protective equipment. "Are you ready to begin?"

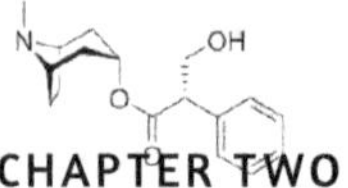

CHAPTER TWO

AUTOPSIES

TANGIER, MOROCCO
JANUARY 21, 2021

Protected by a jumpsuit, surgeon's hood and mask, and double gloves, Mac separated monkey from man on the autopsy table. He could smell stale blood and early decomposition despite the refrigeration of the bodies.

"I'm planning a full autopsy even though the cause of death seems obvious. Are you willing to assist, Amara?"

"I have observed autopsies before, Doctor MacGregor. I don't mind watching bodies cut open, but how much should I worry about infection despite our protective equipment?"

"Stay two meters away until we know what's going on," Mac said as he surveyed the room. Tile walls and floor, fluorescent illumination, metal tables, large sinks, a rack of saws and dissectors, refrigerated chambers along one wall. The smell of formaldehyde and blood. Air conditioning too cold. It could be a hospital morgue anywhere in the world.

A dictating microphone hung above the autopsy table, and Mac spoke into it to describe what he saw, controlling the on-off switch with his foot.

"Male victim, about thirty-five. Multiple scalp lacerations, with tufts of hair and skin ripped away. Part of the right ear is missing, with tooth marks in the remaining tissue.

The right eye has been torn out of its socket and hangs on the optic nerve and inferior rectus muscle. There is a large defect in the nose most compatible with a bite through the skin and cartilage. The right carotid artery has been lacerated along with the sternomastoid muscle and overlying skin. Blood loss from this vessel was certainly the cause of death. The skin surface elsewhere appears normal. No signs of infection."

Mac reconstructed in his mind the sequence that preceded this deadly pairing of man and monkey. The macaque ripped the man's face and scalp apart, then sank teeth into his neck to tear the carotid artery open and cause death by exsanguination. But why had this usually docile animal displayed such violent behavior? And why had it died even though it carried no signs of external trauma?

Mac removed a large syringe from the instrument rack and plunged its nine-inch needle through the chest wall into the man's heart. Dark blood filled the syringe as he pulled back the plunger. Transferring the liquid to culture containers and specimen vials, he commented, "This will be for viral and bacterial cultures."

Amara's skin color changed to pale grey.

"Are you sure you're OK?" he asked. "I can get through this alone if you have to leave."

She shook her head but looked away as he picked up a saw and cut through the man's sternum. Using a scalpel, he extended the incision in an inverted Y into the abdominal region, cut through the abdominal muscle layers in one slice, fit the blades of a large metal retractor under the skin edges, and forced them apart. The central structures of the body came into view: heart and lungs above diaphragm, stomach, intestines, and other abdominal organs below. "Peritoneum, pleura, and internal organs carry no evidence of infection," he noted as he selected tissue fragments and bagged them for further analysis.

A loud voice speaking in Arabic interrupted Mac's concentration. Although he did not understand the words, Mac guessed what the man was clamoring about. Business suit, polished leather shoes, slicked black hair. *Administrator* in any language.

Amara answered in rapid-fire Arabic, translating briefly for Mac after each volley.

"We are official police investigators," she said.

"But no one cleared this procedure with me," the man said. "And our pathologist is away."

"This could not wait," Amara said. "And you know the law. We have the right to use any public facility for urgent police business."

"This is highly irregular." The red-faced administrator moved toward the table.

Mac extended his arm with his palm out. "Not another step!" he barked.

"Why not?" the man said in broken English.

"Because this monkey may be harboring a contagious disease," Mac replied. "Who are you and what is your position here?"

The man sputtered, "I am Mohamed Hassoun, administrator on call."

"Well, Mr. Hassoun, we're going to finish this autopsy." Hassoun did not seem to understand, and Mac turned to Amara. "Can you explain what I just said?"

"Of course, but shouldn't we—"

"Just translate, please." Mac returned to examining the bowel, took further specimens, and waited while Zadi moderated the expletives that came from Hassoun. "Tell him the palace will make his life miserable if he interferes," Mac added.

Hassoun left, muttering curses to himself.

"What did he say?" Mac asked.

"He is going to check with the authorities, namely my boss Duroc."

"Good. That should give us time to finish the autopsy," Mac said. "One other thing we must do for completeness. Stand back. This can be unpleasant." He smoothed the surface of the stomach and cut through it with a large X.

Half-digested food spilled out, with couscous and lamb fragments still evident and foul fumes bursting from the opening.

"What's this?" he asked, picking a small plastic card from the stomach contents.

"Looks like an SD card," Amara said, "But that's impossible."

Mac cleaned it and held it up to the light with tweezers. "How would it get here?"

"Maybe our victim was holding it between his lips and gulped it down by accident?"

"I don't think so. He would have to swallow it deliberately."

Mac handed over the centimeter-square Secure Digital memory device. "Please ask your team to find out if any images can be recovered from it."

"Wouldn't the stomach acid destroy it?"

"Perhaps. Let's find out."

He closed the man's body incisions and scalp using skin-colored stitches, pushed the eye back in its socket, sutured the lid, and returned the corpse to the cooler.

"Now the monkey," Mac said as he put the macaque in a plastic bag. "For that, we'll have to do an operating room transplant. Can you get the OR supervisor down here?"

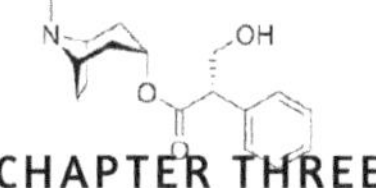

CHAPTER THREE

THE EXPLODING AMYGDALA

The supervisor appeared minutes later, wearing a gown and mask. She stood at the door of the autopsy room and asked Mac what he wanted, speaking in heavily accented English.

"Headlight and craniotome," Mac said. Amara translated into Arabic and a rapid interchange followed. "She can give you a flashlight, brace and bit, and disposable surgical kit. She needs all her other surgical equipment for living patients," Amara said.

Mac decided not to push the issue. If this turned out to be an infection, all instruments he used would have to be quarantined for weeks. Probably better to do the autopsy with crude but disposable instruments.

He turned the monkey's head to the left. Perching on an autopsy stool, he draped the head as he would a human patient and opened a question-mark-shaped incision in front of the right ear. Mac could feel Amara's eyes riveted on him as he held the skin and muscle open and bit away the bone with autopsy rongeurs. He looked carefully at the lining of the brain. "No cloudiness of the meninges

23

to suggest infection," he said, "We'll send off fragments for culture anyway."

He touched the covering of the brain gently. "The brain is very tense."

He used scissors to open the tough lining that covers the cerebral hemispheres. Grey ooze erupted from the opening and continued to flow into the operative field for several seconds. Suction removed the liquefied gray matter and created a path through the temporal lobe. Mac handed the suctioned material to Amara. "The brain has been changed to mush by whatever happened deeper inside. This material should still be OK for culture."

He scooped a final specimen. "And we'll use this tissue for genetic analysis. I suppose we could be looking at a mutant macaque whose genes led to uncontrolled violence, but that explanation seems far-fetched."

He continued as if he were teaching a medical student brain anatomy. "We're entering what should be the lateral ventricle. We'll need to identify the amygdala."

He paused. "Except the amygdala has exploded. Look at this hemorrhage. All I see is blood and fragments of brain."

"What did this?" Amara asked.

"No sign of a blood vessel abnormality such as an arteriovenous malformation. Perhaps it was an increase in blood flow that ruptured an blood vessel."

"Because of a drug?" Amara asked.

"Perhaps. We'll take blood samples for later analysis. Do you have a deep freezer we can use to store blood until I send for it?"

"We can claim a section of one of the freezers here and keep the specimens protected. Just let me know when you want them."

Mac handed her two small vials of blood. "These should stay at minus eighteen degrees. How're you holding up?"

"It's not easy, but it's better than sitting at a desk."

"You might think differently after what I do next. Can you bring me the bucket over there?" He nodded his head toward a covered plastic pail sitting under the sink. "If it smells terrible, it's the container we're looking for."

While Amara retrieved the bucket, Mac used the power saw to cut through scalp and bone around the monkey's head just above the ears. He lifted the top of the skull off like a bowl, slitting the dura with scissors as he did so.

Amara returned with the pail. "This stuff really stinks. Is it what you want?"

Mac leaned over to confirm the unpleasant odor of formalin and nodded.

He turned back to the monkey. With his scissors, he sliced through the optic nerves, spinal cord, and other structures that connect the brain with the rest of the body, then severed the carotid and vertebral arteries. He lifted the entire brain out of the skull, depositing it in the container and sealing the bucket. "We'll save this for a complete brain analysis, but we've already seen a significant finding, the massive amygdala hemorrhage."

Mac proceeded to complete the autopsy of the primate's body, describing each organ for the record. "Viscera and extremities normal," he summarized. "The most striking finding is the bleeding into the amygdala. This monkey died from a brain hemorrhage."

He switched off the microphone and turned to Amara. "The next step is up to you. Can you have the SD card analyzed as fast as possible? Something bizarre is happening. This card holds our only clue."

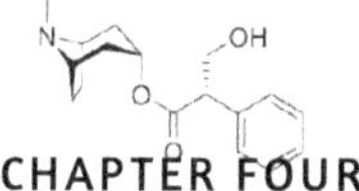

CHAPTER FOUR

THE MONKEY CAGE

TANGIER, MOROCCO
JANUARY 23, 2021

Two days later, Zadi asked Mac to come to a conference room at Tangier's *Villa Dar Jbila* Hotel. Mac expected the typical Western fluorescent-lit conference room with large table and corporate chairs. Instead, he was delighted to see elegantly tiled arches, sheer muslin window treatments, and wall paintings of Moroccan street scenes. The fragrance of jasmine wafted through the open windows that led to the garden.

"You've arranged a great meeting place," Mac said to Amara, who sat at a small tile-surfaced table with a laptop in front of her. "But why aren't we at the police station?"

"Because something is not right. When Prefect Duroc realized we had taken an SD card from the dead man, he confiscated it as evidence but refused to perform any analysis. He said it would be a waste of time and money. And yesterday the card disappeared."

"But, since you invited me here, I assume you had a chance to look at it before he confiscated it?"

"Yes," she nodded and smiled. "More important, one of my tech-savvy friends analyzed it and made a copy. Here's what we found."

A panel on the wall slid back to reveal an LED screen. As Amara started the video, Mac could make out a monkey cage about eight feet square in the center of a large room. The video was spotty because stomach acid had damaged some of it. The viewpoint also jerked and jiggled, as if the photographer could not stabilize the camera. Mac guessed the photographer had placed a phone in the front pocket of a jacket with the camera lens showing, then let the camera run. Whoever it was did not want to be caught videoing the event.

In the foreground of the scene, a large water bottle was anchored on the outside of the cage, with a spout poking through the meshwork. Monkeys lined up to get water at the spout; Mac counted six adults and two infants. A second container provided food at each push of a lever.

As Mac tried to reconstruct the room in his mind, a figure in traditional Arab garb walked to the water dispenser and dumped in powder from a tin. His face could not be seen.

The largest macaque came to the container and drank from it. He sat back, licking his lips as the other males and then females, nursing mothers first, took their turns in apparent rank order. As alpha male, he maintained order and governed the colony.

"You don't need to see the next fifteen minutes," Amara said. "It's just more of the same, a good example of primate socialization. I'm going to fast forward."

Mac's eyes remained fixed on the screen as the video resumed at normal speed.

Without any apparent precipitating event, the large macaque stretched to his full height, bellowed, headed toward a nursing mother, and grabbed her by the neck. He ripped the baby from her and tried to strangle her.

Three other monkeys tried to pull him off, but he kept them at bay with snarling teeth and ferocious roars. Other macaques began to join the altercation. The camera lens turned away from the enclosure and showed two indistinct figures, one in Arab robes, the other in western jeans. Neither person's face could be discerned. In the distance a videographer could be seen recording the events with a professional camera.

By the time the video returned to the focus on the cage, the fight had progressed to become a deadly free-for-all. Animals pulled each other off the walls of the cage, biting off chunks of fur, scalp, tail, and limbs. Their screams and yowls sounded much like human voices, rising in pitch and intensity as the fighting progressed. The alpha male hurled himself at one cellmate, sank his fangs into the animal's neck, and did not release even when spurting blood covered him. The camera caught the two men across from the photographer taking notes as they stepped back.

The alpha macaque threw the body to the floor while fending off bites and blows. He grabbed another animal by the arm and swung him into the cage wall. The crack of breaking bone was accompanied by sudden flaccidity of the victim, dead with a crushed skull.

Mauling, strangling, bellowing, the animals continued their rampage for several minutes. Then the screaming and babbling died away. The floor of the enclosure was filled with blood and corpses.

The door to the cage opened. Fragments of video showed limp monkey bodies and torn limbs being thrown onto a cart. No sound accompanied the erratic images. There was no movement until one monkey lifted his head briefly above the debris that covered him, then lay back down in the carnage. That monkey appeared to be the alpha male.

The video images bounced and changed as if the camera lens moved with the videographer's body. At one point they flipped to display only the wire roof of the cage. *The phone must have fallen out of the videographer's pocket,* Mac thought.

A face appeared in the screen, getting larger as the subject looked at the camera lens, presumably to pick up his phone. Mac drew in a breath. Amara gasped at the same time. Mac knew why.

The man taking the video was the man they had just autopsied.

The recording stopped abruptly. Mac sat motionless, realizing that he had been holding his breath and staring through most of the slaughter. He blinked and looked over at Amara.

She shook her head. "Can you explain to me what happened there? I grew up with macaques. They never act like this. The most aggressive they get is to steal something from a sack. What did the robed man put in that water?"

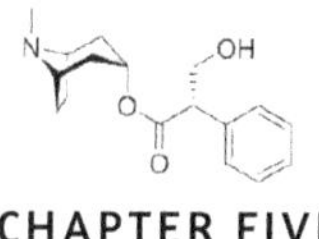

BERSERKER POWDER

TANGIER, MOROCCO
JANUARY 23, 2021

The room seemed smaller and darker, and Mac could almost smell the blood and dismembered flesh he had just seen. Amara wrung her hands, more agitated than she had been during the autopsy.

He took a moment to collect his thoughts. "Nothing in the external environment provoked this. The powder in the water must have changed some chemistry in the animal's brain."

"Do you agree that the monkey you autopsied is the one that was still moving at the end of the video?" Amara asked.

"Yes, and the man we just autopsied was the videographer," Mac said.

"Which brings me to the other reason we're meeting in a hotel and not at the police station," Amara said. "I tried to get M. Duroc to run our victim's fingerprints through the Interpol registry when he first came in. He said there was no need to do that."

"But you did it anyway?" Mac was beginning to learn how to anticipate Amara's actions. She did what he would have done in her situation.

"Yes. I have a friend in Rabat who submitted them for me."

"And?" Mac asked.

"And you will be upset by what I found."

"Which is?" Mac's impatience became evident.

"Our victim was not really an animal attendant. He was an Interpol agent in the international terrorism division."

Mac let the information sink in. He now understood why a man killed by a berserk monkey would be of interest to Jim Brogan and the CIA.

He addressed Amara with an intense stare. "Amara, please keep this information to yourself. You should not talk to anyone about this, certainly not to Duroc. You've done great work, but I don't think you should continue. Too dangerous."

"After what we just saw? Can you imagine what would happen if the material in that water got into a crowd of humans rather than a colony of monkeys? I want to keep going, Duroc or no Duroc."

"Do you understand how dangerous it could be?"

"I want to stay on the case. I can work in the background if necessary. What do you need most?"

"The location of that monkey facility, but the CIA and I can work that out."

"I can do it faster. I'll find out who the telephone numbers on the SD card belong to and see if there's a warehouse among them."

"I have to make a couple of calls," Mac said.

Seeking open space and absence of surveillance, he

descended the tile staircase to the verdant garden between the hotel and the Mediterranean. Moroccan daisies lined the path, in full bloom in the sixty-degree January weather. Chrysanthemums and clematis added their colorful blossoms. Sculpted boxwood hedgerows created an atmosphere of cultivated elegance.

Mac's first call went to Jim Brogan, the CIA colleague who had asked Mac to drop everything and go to Tangier. "I want to be sure this is not a new virus infecting the monkey," Brogan had said as he put the request to Mac. "Sending a platoon of CDC doctors would create world-wide panic. As a single physician, you can investigate quietly, get brain and blood specimens, and help us sort out whether a macaque attacked and killed a man because it was infected with a new virus."

Brogan must have suspected all along that this was not a virus and that Interpol was involved. Putting together the clandestine monkey facility and the powder in the water which produced deadly rage, Mac concluded some new bio-terrorism weapon was likely the concern.

As he waited for the call to connect, Mac felt mounting annoyance at being misled. When Brogan answered, he began without the usual niceties. "Jim, Mac here. I assume you knew this Moroccan problem wasn't a virus."

"Whoa there, Mac. What have you found?" Brogan said.

"I want to know what's in the powder."

"Powder? What powder?"

"The powder that makes monkeys insanely aggressive."

"So the problem is definitely not an infection?"

Mac paused. Perhaps he had jumped to conclusions too quickly.

"Mac, are you there? Can you tell me what you've found?" Brogan asked.

"No infection, but a video that is intensely disturbing. It shows a powder dissolved in drinking water that makes monkeys berserk. And the man who took the video worked for Interpol. What's really going on, Jim? It's time for the truth."

Brogan hesitated a moment, then seemed to come to a decision and spoke rapidly. "The dead man is Khaled Medan, an Interpol agent in the terrorism group covering Africa. He discovered that an American company was testing a compound that produces rage, got a position as an animal attendant in the manufacturing facility, and said he would obtain a video that demonstrated the effects of the drug." Brogan's voice trailed off. "That's when we lost contact with him."

"We just saw the video he made. What the compound does is indescribable. And we have independent confirmation that this man really was Khaled."

"We?" Brogan asked.

"I'm working with a young police officer named Amara Zadi. Do you know her?"

"Not personally. I've coordinated our efforts through Duroc, the chief of police in Tangier."

"Duroc is not trustworthy."

"He certainly has been uncooperative. Mac, I apologize if you believe I got you to Tangier under false pretenses. Can you track down the location of the facility with the monkey colony? It may be the storehouse for the chemical as well as its manufacturing site. We need to find out who's making the compound and what they intend to do. That chemical must not be released on the world."

"I'll work on it for a couple of days, but not much longer. I have to get back to my family."

"Let me know what you find. And thanks." Brogan disconnected the call.

Looking at the flowers and trees around him, Mac thought of the snow he had left behind in Boston. Was he deliberately trying to run away from winter?

He called home. Both his eight-year-old son Peter and twelve-year-old daughter Maggie were doing school from the house because of COVID-19. His wife Lauren, a teacher at a prominent Boston school for girls, also did her teaching from home now.

Waiting for the WhatsApp call to connect, he considered the fact that the rest of his family was safer without him. As a front-line health care worker, he had been doubly vaccinated against the virus as soon as Massachusetts allowed it. He had also gotten a severe form of the infection in Wuhan, China, a year ago, but he knew that did not keep him from spreading the virus. His exposure to patients and his travel made him the most dangerous person in the family bubble. He had a hard time dealing with that reality.

He chatted with each child and with Lauren, feeling acutely the gap that separated them. Even in Boston, he could not interact comfortably with them, had to be careful of physical contact, wear a mask if he thought he had been particularly at risk at work.

"I'll be back in a day or two," he said as he hung up, cursing the virus and what it had done to the family relationships. He felt as disconnected as the phone.

Amara brought him out of his self-recriminations. Waving from the window, she called with triumph in her voice, "I found it."

When Mac returned to the conference room, she showed him the address and phone number of a company called Amygdalin. "I thought it was a bizarre name until I remembered what you told me the amygdala does. It's the part of the brain that generates anger impulses, right? After that video, I understand the company name only too well."

"We should try to visit the warehouse to get more information," Mac said. "But we'll need to do it with police protection. I will talk to M. Duroc."

Duroc resisted. When Mac threatened to get Interpol and the national Moroccan authorities involved, the prefect agreed to visit the warehouse but said it would take a few hours to arrange everything.

Three hours later, Mac bumped and swayed in an all-terrain police vehicle driven by Amara toward the outskirts of Tangier. A Kevlar vest chafed against his armpits. Duroc and a colleague drove ahead of them in a jeep, sirens blazing and sand plumes rising into the afternoon sky.

"Monsieur Duroc does not appear to believe in subtlety in his investigation," Mac shouted as they careened from one side of the unpaved highway to another.

"Tangier is a small city. Everyone would know what we're doing even if we crept up to the building in the middle of the night," Amara replied.

They turned off the road and followed a well-worn double track, bouncing violently along the potholes left by winter rain. The path ended in front of a large building without windows sitting well back from the road. A couple of plain white vans sat in the clearing outside the structure, but no signs betrayed its ownership.

The group assembled in front of Duroc's vehicle. "I will go first, then tell you when it is safe," Duroc said. He walked to the door and rang the bell, with Mac and Amara a few feet behind. "The door is unlocked," he shouted. "Maybe they are expecting us."

He stepped into the building.

The flash blinded Mac. Instinctively, he threw himself in front of Amra to protect her. The blast that followed hurled both of them to the ground. Mac's world crashed to black.

CHAPTER SIX

MORLOCK

"So how do you justify destroying our Morocco facility?" Rufus Morlock threw the question at his *consigliere* Steve Therman with the same energy he used to pound the punching bag in front of him. In his seventies, Morlock maintained body weight and strength by working out regularly in his personal gym on top of his Sixth Avenue skyscraper.

Morlock had arrived in the United States as an impoverished immigrant and created a media empire that upended American politics. His Right TV network, newspaper chain, and links to conservative politicians produced a phalanx of disinformation difficult to match.

He did not tolerate obstacles. Right now, he was furious that his Moroccan warehouse had exploded. His accelerated heart rate, forehead sweat, and tightened muscles sublimated his anger. The gym machines and mats, stench of sweat, and sound of landed blows on the punching bag released his frustrations as well as kept him in shape.

He paused to hear Therman's response.

"Two words," Therman replied. "Duncan MacGregor."

"Who the hell is that?"

"A Boston neurosurgeon who suddenly appeared in Morocco. We think the CIA sent him. He has a talent for sticking his nose where it doesn't belong. We had no choice but to blow the facility up. He and his associates were getting too close."

"Even though the plant had all our product in it as well as the equipment and personnel for further production?" Morlock felt his heart rate increase even further.

"I know how you must feel," Therman said. "I had as much riding on that plant as you. Remember, I'm the guy who created the facility in the first place. And in case you don't recall, I also stole the Viking orb for you, got the Berserker powder inside it analyzed, and hired the chemists to improve on it. My whole life has been tied up with Berserker for the last two years."

"In no way can you know how I feel," Morlock said, switching from the heavy bag to the small repeating one. "It was my idea to use this powder to destabilize social systems and pave the way for strong leaders. In any case, I'm sure you realize you're only as useful as your last job." His thick silver hair became slick with sweat as he hammered away. "How exactly did MacGregor muck up the works?"

"He got his hands on an SD card containing videos of the experiments we did on the monkeys," Therman replied.

"How did the card get into his hands?"

"One of our animal assistants turned out to be an Interpol agent. He took the videos without our knowledge and swallowed the SD card. MacGregor found it during the autopsy after the man was killed by a macaque. It forced a raid on the plant. How could we anticipate that?"

"What about the other workers? Did any of them survive your explosion?"

"Yes. Duroc warned us the place was about to be raided. Even then, we only had two hours to prepare for the attack. We couldn't get the powder out in time."

"Were any employees killed?"

"No important ones. Duroc and his deputy died. Just as well. And MacGregor was hurt along with a Moroccan policewoman."

"Can we eliminate MacGregor while he's recovering?"

"If he's kept in the hospital, I believe we could. We still have a lot of Moroccan cops on our payroll."

"Can the employees who survived the explosion rebuild the facility?"

"Yes, and we don't need many people now. The whole process has been automated."

"And where will the new plant be?"

"On our container ship *Sakinah*. We were going to use it to distribute the compound anyway. It'll now be a floating manufacturing facility and animal test site as well as transport ship. We've modified eight containers to make them mini-pharmaceutical plants. On a ship, we can keep moving so no one will be able to track us down. We'll also have the capability to distribute to any major port in the world."

"How about the workers? Isn't it a problem to keep them quiet about this?"

"We only need a crew of about twenty including a couple of engineers to make sure the processing goes smoothly. Most of the workers have no idea what we're creating. The only person besides me who knows exactly what we're doing is Erfan Hameni, who can be trusted completely."

"And you're confident we're making active product?"

"The monkey testing facility assures our drug is bioactive. When a new batch is made, we add the compound to the macaques' drinking water and watch them go berserk. We're also going to test it out at Carnival in Rio in three weeks. Fortunately, we sent the special water bottles to Brazil before the Morocco problem."

Morlock stopped hammering the punching bag and added, "You guarantee we'll be ready to distribute the powder around the world by July fourth?"

"I would prefer to use it in the United States first."

"You have no say in this. You make the stuff. I decide where it goes."

Morlock placed his sweaty face millimeters from Therman's and released the full force of his stale breath. "And you'd better have the powder ready, because if you are not on schedule at our next meeting, that will be the last meeting you ever see. Now get the hell out of here and get to your work before I find someone who can do it better."

CHAPTER SEVEN

MAC RECOVERS

TANGIER, MOROCCO
JANUARY 23-26, 2021

Mac forced his eyes open. The odor of burnt flesh filled his nostrils. The hiss of flaming grass and shrubs replaced the thunderclap that had hit him with its shock wave. When he tried to move, his right leg erupted with pain.

He lay on his back, head partly embedded in sand. Helmet gone. Face red from the blast's burn. Blood on his fingers when he rubbed his cheeks or scalp. Smoldering debris and sand spattered on his burnt Kevlar vest. Heart racing and head confused.

Duroc. Where is Duroc? And Amara! Is she alive? The fear that he had led his young companion to her death broke over him like a wave. He called out her name, but no sound came. Eyes swollen shut, he explored the sand, shrubs, and grass around him with his hands, seeking human contact. He tried to sit up. Excruciating pain rocketed through his body, beginning with the right leg. The world faded again.

When Mac woke the second time, he lay in a cool bed with an intravenous catheter in his left arm, oxygen prongs in his nose, and splint elevating his right leg. His eyes and face were bandaged. He moved, groaning, to adjust to a more comfortable position.

"Dr. Mac?" Amara's voice came from close by.

"Amara? Is that you? Are you OK?" Mac's voice squeaked and rasped.

"I am so happy you are awake. You saved my life. How can I thank you?"

"What happened?" Mac asked.

"The building exploded. Duroc and the officer with him were killed. You jumped in front of me to protect me from the blast, and you were knocked out. I crawled away and called in for help. You're at Hassan V hospital now. You have fractured your right fibula and have many burns and cuts, but the doctors say you will heal."

"Does my family know?"

"No. I couldn't open your phone."

"How long have I been out?"

"About four hours. Everyone was worried about you."

"Any more information on the blast?" Mac's head throbbed with every movement.

"No. I think the owners got the message that it was going to be raided."

"What time is it?"

"Two p.m."

Eight a.m. in Boston. "Is my phone charged?" Mac tried to sit up, fell back against pillows.

"Use mine." Amara pressed it into his hand.

Mac called his wife's cell but got only voicemail.

He decided to call his landline but couldn't remember

the number for the moment. He passed the phone to Amara and asked her to try several combinations. On the fourth, she returned it to him with his daughter Maggie answering. "Hello? Who is this?"

"It's Daddy. Can you put Mommy on the phone?"

"Daddy! When are you coming back? Your voice sounds all weird. We had a big snowstorm today. I got an A in my science project."

"I'm coming home as soon as I can. Is Mommy there?"

"She's talking to Nana."

"Can you interrupt her?" Mac waited a few seconds, lying back on the pillows.

"Mac?" Lauren sounded strained. "What's going on?"

"I had an accident."

"What kind of accident? Were you hurt?"

"Some scrapes, and I broke my right fibula. That's a supporting part of the leg—no big deal."

"Was it a car accident? Were you driving?"

"No. I'll tell you everything as soon as I get home."

"I want to know now, Mac. Tell me what happened."

"A warehouse blew up in front of me. I must have hit my leg on a rock and broke the bone. Don't worry about it. With a splint, I'll be able to do everything."

"A warehouse blew up? Mac, what are you talking about? What are you doing there? Can you stop please? Can you come home now?"

"I'll be home as soon as the doctors let me travel."

"When is that going to be?"

"I'll WhatsApp you as soon as I know."

"Please make it soon."

"Of course. I love you."

The effort of talking exhausted him, and he drifted to sleep.

The Moroccan orthopedist standing by Mac's bed the next morning seemed both competent and adamant. "You should not travel for two weeks and would be best to stay in the hospital."

"It's only a fibular fracture," Mac countered. "I don't need to be in a hospital for two weeks for a fracture that will heal on its own. My family needs me, and I need them."

"But the leg will be very painful," the orthopod said. "If you don't rest it, the bone may go on to non-union."

Amara interrupted. "I have the solution. Dr. Mac will stay at our home while the fracture heals. Our housemen will take care of him. We can teach him to walk with a splint."

"I already have a hotel room," Mac said.

"A hotel is no place to recover from your injuries. I'm not sure the hospital is safe," Amara said. "I feel responsible for what happened to you and worry about something more going wrong. I have talked to my parents, and they insist. When you save a Moroccan's life, you become part of her family. You would dishonor us to refuse."

Later that day, Mac hobbled out of a limousine with Amara at his side, trying his best to maneuver with crutches as they approached her house. Solid gray plastered walls surrounded the compound except for a wooden door, with a visible video camera on its door frame.

Amara punched in a code and spoke Arabic at the intercom. A manservant appeared at the door and guided them along the path leading to the main building.

The interior was spectacularly different than the exterior. A well-tended garden with lush grass, flowers, and trees surrounded them. Clusters of dates dangled like grapes from the branches of the palms. Oranges and clementines hung from other trees scattered on the lawn. The fragrance of citrus and jasmine permeated the internal space. Afternoon sun dappled the grass.

Inside the house itself, Amara introduced her father, a man in his fifties wearing a business suit and a mask. He welcomed Mac in Oxford English. "You are part of our family now that you have saved my daughter's life. I can never repay you for that."

He described the organization of the house and accompanied Mac's elevator to a second-floor bedroom. "We have central heating and air conditioning, and your room has its own climate controls. Please set the temperature where you wish. We also use 4G internet, password *Amara*. If you need anything at all, just ring the bell. Our man will take care of you."

Mac unpacked quickly in the luxurious room, made the more elegant by exquisite tile work and whitewashed walls. He visited the bathroom, noted the bidet, soaking tub, and large stall with rain shower, then returned exhausted to the duvet-covered bed. He took a moment to inhale the scents of orange and mixed floral bouquets wafting through the arched window. Rarely had he felt so much at home in such unfamiliar surroundings.

He wanted to get up and continue his investigation. Instead, he drifted off to sleep.

He woke the next morning to find Amara sitting in a chair beside him.

"Good morning," Mac said, "Or is it morning? I have no idea how long I've been sleeping."

"It's nine a.m. How are you feeling?"

"Still wiped out, and my right leg hurts a lot," Mac said, remembering the events that preceded his injury. "Did you find out who owns the warehouse?"

"No success," she reported. "The registered company is just a shell. We did find a reason for Duroc's resistance to our investigation. An anonymous source has been placing regular sums of money in his bank account for months, more than doubling his salary. Obviously, a payoff for something."

"Good work."

"And there's something else," Amara continued. "I couldn't wipe the video of that man Khaled loading monkey carcasses into a wheelbarrow out of my mind. He would have to dispose of the monkey bodies within a few miles of the warehouse. I followed the road and came across a site covered with fresh dirt about a mile from the explosion. We'll be digging it up in an hour. Would you like to join us?"

"I don't think I'm up to it. Can you link me in with WhatsApp video?"

An hour later Mac began to receive images from Amara's phone. The site she had chosen showed freshly disturbed sand. After a few minutes of digging, she transmitted the image of a macaque paw grasping another monkey's ear.

"This is certainly the place. The stench is horrible," Amara reported. "The monkey corpses are starting to rot."

The camera shifted to show an infant and a nursing mother with her face half clawed off. "Here's what we have uncovered so far," Amara said.

Mac sat silent, contemplating the horror that must have taken place in the cage in the warehouse. The video they had watched did not do justice to the bloody, mutilating violence necessary to produce that burial scene.

"What should I do next?" Amara asked. "My superiors don't seem to care about this monkey massacre. They say they are too busy dealing with the problems of the city to worry about macaques. And several of them are now fighting for Duroc's position."

"I need to get the CIA involved to track down the real warehouse owners. I hope we can find them before whatever they are planning gets released on humans."

From his guest room Mac talked with Jim Brogan, who promised to investigate the ghost companies behind the warehouse but said it might take several days.

While he waited, Mac pushed himself to walk, learned to navigate the stairs, and spent time limping through the beautiful garden behind the home. Three days after his arrival at Amara's home, he persuaded his orthopedist to allow him to fly back to Boston. Amara's parents insisted on a banquet in his honor the evening before he left.

Twelve relatives and friends sat around a large table placed in the garden. Mac sat at the center, with Amara on his left and her father to his right. Amara's mother, who spoke only halting English, sat across from them. They had all discarded their masks.

As guests began to reach for hors d'oeuvres and eye their Moroccan grey wine, Amara's father proposed a toast to Mac as "my new brother." He introduced each member of the group, which included family members but also wealthy merchants, politicians, and representatives of the king.

Mixed olives with harissa and roasted eggplant and yogurt preceded carrot soup. Pastilla came next, proudly presented by the cook and several helpers. "Real pigeon, not chicken," Amara commented as Mac savored the delicate pastry and flavorful meat. Servers cleared the preliminaries and entered with the main course, lamb tagine with cumquats.

The diners peeled portions off the roast lamb by using unleavened bread as their forks. Mac felt awkward at first but soon enjoyed the process of sharing. Couscous under the lamb, chickpea salad, and Moroccan sweet potatoes accompanied the main course. Delightful Moroccan red wine, a mixture of Syrah and other grapes, accompanied the perfectly cooked meat.

Now the servers brought in bowls of fruit—oranges, clementines, pomegranates, grapes, and apples. Mint tea helped wash down the final dessert—cookies with sesame seeds. The entire meal took three hours, and Mac could hardly follow the French, Arabic, and Berber fragments of conversation bouncing back and forth around him. Almost everyone switched from one language to another without

hesitation. The only exception was English, which most diners did not speak fluently.

The fresh Mediterranean air, jasmine flowers, and savory
spices created a complex olfactory mix that Mac would
remember for a long time. The sound of multiple languages,
birds chirping in the trees, the visual delight of garden and
late afternoon sun; all these made for a sense of community
Mac reveled in. He participated as vigorously as he could
and was amazed by the cultural sophistication and genuine
camaraderie he witnessed around him. He had truly been
adopted by this family and felt completely welcome.

The host ended the meeting by passing cold water around
and standing for one final toast. "My brother, we wish you
safe voyage back to Boston. I also want to offer our Paris
condominium to you this summer. It is in a lovely street in
the first arrondissement. Amara will pester you about the
dates until you accept and confirm. Please plan to take at
least a week to enjoy our flat, and know we are forever grateful to you."

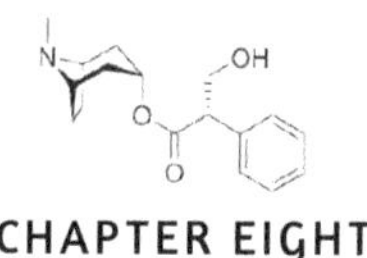

CHAPTER EIGHT

SEARCHING FOR A LEADER

"And where is Duncan MacGregor right now?" Max Eli asked the faces on the ZOOM screen before him. "Wasn't he supposed to be back a week ago?" Eli was chief of neurology at Harbor Hospital and had successfully maneuvered to become chair of the new committee to select a chief of neurosurgery.

His goal was to weaken Duncan MacGregor's candidacy. *It's not jealousy,* he thought before he spoke to the committee members. *It's tactics.* He knew that MacGregor had academic credibility, international recognition, and capacity to support Harbor Hospital programs. If Mac became chief of the new neurosurgery department, his would be the dominant neuroscience voice in the hospital hierarchy. Eli would become second-best, with neuro programs controlled by a neurosurgeon.

"Mac has been delayed in Morocco," Julia Pedroza said from the screen.

Eli groaned. Pedroza was the only Hispanic member of the committee and the elected representative of the neurosurgical service. Her voice could not be ignored, especially

51

since she had been appointed to the committee by the medical school.

"It isn't the first time Mac's been missing in action," Eli said to hammer his point home. "Last year, as I recall, he disappeared in Wuhan, China. And our search for a chairman has to go beyond Duncan MacGregor. We're charged to find the best candidate in the world."

He signaled Rose Jackson, the committee representative from Human Resources who he had coached before the meeting. "Rose, can you describe the background to the search?"

"Neurosurgery is presently a division of general surgery at Harbor Hospital," Rose said. "It has grown big enough to become its own department, which requires an official search for a chief. As a department, it will have a major voice in the management of the hospital."

"And can you tell us what kind of person we're looking for?" Eli asked, hoping she would name qualities that would diminish MacGregor's suitability.

"Someone who has the respect of colleagues around the world, is collaborative, available, and fiscally responsible, and believes in a diverse work force."

Julia Pedroza raised her hand on the ZOOM screen. "I want to point out that Dr. MacGregor fulfills all those criteria. He has recruited diverse staff like me. He has collaborated with other groups like neuropathology, neuroradiology, and neurology and has supported their budgets. Through his international travels and teaching, he has become one of the most respected neurosurgeons in the world."

"Thank you," Eli said, clenching his fists below the visible camera frame.

"I'm not finished," Pedroza continued. "Some of the requirements Rose mentions are mutually contradictory. Take world respect and availability. International respect requires lecturing in other countries. It can't be earned by sitting at Harbor Hospital attending meetings."

"Thank you again, Dr. Pedroza," Eli said. *When would this woman shut up?*

"I'm still not finished. Dr. MacGregor is the logical choice as chief, considering his world reputation and familiarity with our hospital culture. Couldn't we just put his name forward and be done?"

"We have to follow the process of vetting many candidates," Eli replied, turning away from the screen to hide his rising anger. He turned again to Rose, "Can you elaborate on fiscal responsibility as a requirement?"

"Neurosurgery has traditionally supported other specialties financially, especially pediatrics and trauma surgery. The new chief should continue this support."

"May I remind the group that this policy was initiated by Dr. MacGregor?" Pedroza said.

"And availability?" Eli asked, hoping that Mac would fail at least this criterion.

"The hospital wants a person in this position who will attend meetings regularly, enhancing our culture of collegiality and togetherness," Rose replied.

"I assume that means being here in Boston," Eli said. "Is that an absolute requirement?"

"Nothing is absolute, but the institution would prefer a presence here."

"May I interrupt?" the chief of neuroradiology asked.

"Of course," Eli said, glad to hear from someone other than Julia.

"I'm not good at hospital politics, but since Dr. MacGregor has led the division of neurosurgery at Harbor Hospital our surgical cases have quadrupled. This has allowed us to join world leaders in brain imaging."

"Which means?" Eli asked.

"I agree with Dr. Pedroza that we could just save time and recommend MacGregor."

"Thank you. Any other comments?" *Maybe I should just stop the meeting.*

The psychiatrist unmuted himself. "I hear there's a great young neurosurgeon at Boston General named Gorman. Could we recruit him? That would also lessen our competition in Boston."

"That's the kind of suggestion we need," Eli said. "Could each of you send me names of possible candidates between now and next meeting? Thank you for joining us today."

In the private ZOOM chat box, Eli asked Pedroza to stay behind. "Julia, it's premature to suggest Mac should be the chief," he said after the other members had signed off.

"No one in the country comes close to his talent and reputation."

"I'm surprised you're willing to follow him. I would have thought a capable woman like you might be more independent in her thinking."

"I'm independent all right, just not in agreement with you. But I can't stay any longer. I have to get back to patients," Pedroza said, and disappeared from the screen.

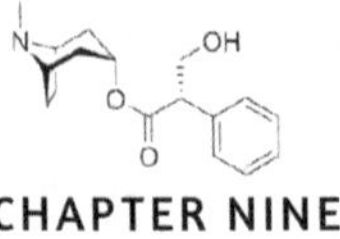

CHAPTER NINE

MAC RETURNS TO BOSTON

BOSTON, MA
JANUARY 31, 2021

Mac's return to Boston went as smoothly as could be expected for someone with a broken leg. Amara Zadi's father insisted on providing first class passage, claiming that "the plane is an extension of our house. You must be comfortable, which means stretching out with your leg up. I will take care of everything."

At the transfer in Charles de Gaulle airport, a representative of the Moroccan embassy met Mac at the gate and rolled him through the airport in a wheelchair. Mac felt embarrassed. The man assured him that many VIP skiers returning from the French Alps needed the same assistance.

On the plane, Mac slept the entire seven hours from Paris to Boston despite the entertainment and food available in his first-class cocoon. When he arrived in Boston, an airline representative accompanied him past border control and a porter took his bags to maneuver him through customs and the international arrivals doorway. Mr. Zadi had kept his promise.

Lauren stood waiting behind the rail, pale and apprehensive. "Thank God you're safe," she said as she rushed to give

56

him a hug. "What exactly happened in Tangier? Why were you anywhere near an explosion?"

"Long story. Looks like it has a happy ending, since I'm back with you." He returned her hug with a feeling of tremendous relief that he was back home. On the drive to their Brookline house, he described his ordeal, with emphasis on the kindness of Amara Zadi's family.

Maggie and Peter clustered to him as he hobbled through the front door with crutches. The smiles on their faces made him forget his injuries and almost everything else that had happened in Tangier.

"Were you really in an explosion?" Maggie asked.

"Was it an IED?" Peter asked. "Do you have any shrapnel fragments in your body?"

"What about your leg, Daddy? How can you drive with that splint?" Maggie asked. "Can we go to Morocco some day?"

"Wait a minute," Mac said with a laugh. He could feel endorphins surge through his body at the joy of being with his family again. "Let me sit so I can tell you what happened. But tell me what you've been up to first."

He sat on the couch and put his leg up. "Now," he said, "tell me everything."

"We're learning about France," Maggie said. "I hope someday I can visit Provence and Paris and see Notre Dame and the Eiffel Tower and the Seine. Did you know Notre Dame had a big fire but they're repairing it?"

"I'm learning about Vikings," Peter said. "Some of them wore bear skins and thought they were actual animals.

Because they were crazy violent, they were called Berserkers. That's where our word *berserk* comes from..."

After another hour of continuous update, Mac headed for bed, grateful to be back in the family nest.

His arrival at the hospital the next morning was less joyful. He wanted to continue his investigation of what caused a docile monkey to become hyper-violent, but there were obstacles to that investigation.

Julia Pedroza brought him up to date on his patients. Mac thanked her and the other surgeons who had covered for him. He knew very well he could not do his international work without their help. Julia also reported that the search for a departmental chief had begun, and Max Eli seemed determined to undermine Mac's candidacy.

The clinic administrator called to remind Mac he had left Boston with incomplete patient dictations. He spent the morning catching up on those to avoid being reprimanded. In the next weeks he tried to resume his usual life. Intermittent pain reminded him he would cause permanent damage by not caring for the break. He cut back on his surgical schedule, but continued to teach, carry out lab investigations, and spend as much time as he could with Lauren, Maggie, and Peter.

He also tried without much luck to research drugs that might make docile monkeys go berserk. Realizing he needed help, he turned to Dr. Grace Wu, a neuropathologist and neuroscientist at the hospital who was expert in the circuits of the brain causing uncontrolled anger.

He invited Grace to lunch at The Boston Fish House. The blazing hearth of the harborside restaurant provided a welcome contrast to the freezing wind and whirling snow outside the windows. While Mac downed Wellfleet oysters, Grace dissected her lobster like a native New Englander. "I grew up in Rockport." she said as she saw Mac's admiring glance. "But how can I help you and justify this wonderful lunch?"

"You can explain something I saw while I was in Morocco," Mac replied. "A macaque killed a man. No one there had ever seen a monkey attack a human like that."

"Perhaps a monkey who had been abused?"

"It was in a cage with other macaques. No sign of abuse."

"Could it have been infected? Rabid, maybe?"

"We checked for infection in the autopsy," Mac said. "No signs of inflammation and the cultures were negative." He looked out at the swirling snow. "I think it was a pharmacological substance. We saw someone spike the monkeys' water just before this happened. Could any drug you know make a macaque go wild and then blow up its amygdala?"

"What do you mean by *blow up its amygdala?*"

"The animal had a massive brain hemorrhage that started in its amygdala. No signs of head injury, and no other reason it should have had such a hemorrhage. Could any drug you know cause something like this?"

"Not that comes to mind."

"Could you identify a chemical from a blood sample even after a couple of weeks? I drew two vials of blood from the monkey. It's been kept frozen by a friend in Morocco."

"It's certainly worth testing. Meanwhile, I'll try to track down what pharmacological agent might do what you describe. This sounds like a lot more than a monkey problem. What if the monkeys were just test animals for a new drug that causes violent behavior?"

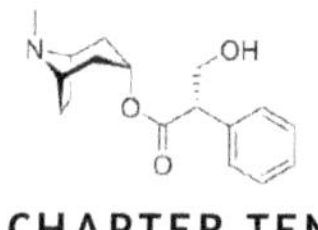

CHAPTER TEN

THE SCIENCE OF RAGE

BOSTON, MA
FEBRUARY 3, 2021

As soon as he returned to the hospital, Mac texted Amara to send the blood samples by DHL. Three days later, Grace reported that she had received the specimens. She called him back the next day, voice tremulous with excitement. "I think I've found the drug. Can you meet me in my office in an hour?"

She greeted Mac with one word as he entered her office.

"Henbane," she said with a triumphant ring, "Henbane. Or some people prefer the name *Stinking nightshade*."

"Henbane? What's that?" Mac echoed as he took a seat.

"A plant used by the ancient Greeks in battle."

"It causes rage?" Mac asked.

Grace nodded. "Yes. And two years ago, a scientist named Karsten Fatur proposed in the Journal of Ethnopharmacology that henbane also explained the violence of Viking Berserkers. These warriors were famous for their aggressive behavior. He suggested that the combination of pain tolerance, visual hallucinations, and enhanced aggression would explain the insane violence these men exhibited. That led me to narrow down my analysis."

"So the drug you found in the blood was henbane? A thousand-year-old Viking compound suddenly reappeared in Morocco to make monkeys violent?" Mac asked.

"Our analysis showed a chemically modified derivative of *Hyoscyamus niger*, or black henbane." Grace turned out the lights and turned on the visual display. An assembly of balls and sticks rotated in the air in front of her as she manipulated her computer.

"This is hyoscyamine, the active molecule in henbane."

She clicked, and the configuration of the molecule changed. Several red balls appeared on the sticks as the whole assembly tilted and cavorted in the darkened room. "And this is the molecule we found in the monkey blood."

"They look the same to me," Mac said

"You're a surgeon. You may not recognize subtle variations in drug configuration. If you look carefully, there are important differences evident on three-dimensional modelling. For one thing, the new configuration will allow the compound to bind to brain receptors more tightly. And it's a lot easier to manufacture," Grace added.

"It has the same effects as henbane?"

"This drug—let's call it Berserker—is more potent. When it binds to the amygdala, it puts the whole brain on red alert."

"Which means?" Mac asked.

"Widespread brain activation. A critical function of the brain is to protect the body against invaders. The amygdala interprets whether a situation is dangerous and initiates the fight or flight response."

"And this drug initiates fight?" Mac asked, now paying full attention.

"Exactly. Under the influence of this drug, the amygdala would warn the rest of the brain that everything in the environment is dangerous." The hologram switched to show a brain rotating around its base. "You might recognize this," Grace said.

"The crown jewel of evolution— the human brain," Mac said. "Three pounds of gray matter with a billion neurons and a trillion supporting cells that make you and me who we are."

"No surprise you got that right," Grace said with a smile. "The important point is there is little general activity in brain neurons—the brain in a resting state."

The hologram changed to a brain almost on fire, with red and yellow fibers stretching to every part of the visible cortex.

Grace continued, "This is what happens when our amygdala signals overwhelming danger. Our frontal lobes become suppressed—we stop listening to reason. Our vision becomes uncertain—we don't see objects for what they really are. Our sensations are distorted—we may think we are flying or have visual hallucinations. All our movements and attention are directed at an aggressive attack against whatever happens to be in front of us."

She changed images. "And this is what the Berserker compound does."

"Looks like just what you described," Mac said.

"Exactly. Activation of the whole brain to fight."

"Would there be any change in brain blood vessels?"

"Why do you ask?"

"The amygdala hemorrhage in the monkey."

"Perhaps. Brain arterioles expand to supply oxygen when there is increased brain activity. It's theoretically possible that they would leak and explode if they were driven too hard."

She turned on the lights and punched at her computer keys. "We can model this right now. Let's suppose the amygdala activation continues for two hours at full strength. I'm going to time lapse the two hours into two minutes."

Mac watched as the amygdala swelled more and more. After sixty seconds, it exploded.

"In the real brain, this amygdala rupture would be accompanied by a hemorrhage that would increase brain pressure and kill the victim. The whole cycle would take about sixty minutes. Does that answer your question?" Grace asked.

"If that happens in the first hour after taking the drug, why didn't all the Berserkers die during battle? Surely their combat took longer than sixty minutes."

Wu flicked the lights on again. "This is where it gets really interesting. The Berserker drug is metabolized by the product of a special gene, a gene that is only found in people of Nordic origin—Danes, Swedes, Norwegians, and their descendants."

"Meaning many people from Great Britain," Mac added, "since the Vikings infiltrated so much of East England."

He stared at Grace as the implications registered with him. "And if you don't have that gene?"

"You've seen the result," she said. "Your amygdala would blow out after an hour. Monkeys don't have it; their amygdalas explode. If a Scot like you took the drug, your

Scandinavian genes would break down the drug so you could continue fighting indefinitely. After two or three hours you would be exhausted but intact. If I took the drug with my Chinese genetic makeup, I would have a fatal brain hemorrhage in an hour."

"How do people know what genes they have?"

"That's the problem, isn't it?" Grace said. "Legend says a few of the Berserkers fell dead even before they started to fight—perhaps they did not have the right genes. Even among Nordic tribes, there was genetic diversity."

"So let me get this straight," Mac said. "We have a powder that causes extreme rage. It turns out to be a modification of a compound that has been known for centuries. It can be fatal in people without the right Nordic genes. Who on earth would want to use such a compound?"

"I can think of lots of people," Grace said, frowning. "Soldiers of Scandinavian countries would be immune. I suppose they could become twenty-first century Berserkers. More important, though, I think white supremacists would grab it. They think they're in a privileged class anyway, protected even if they had a mixed genetic makeup." Grace sounded angry. "I can imagine them putting this compound in a city's water to incite uncontrollable riots, blame Antifa or whoever, and declare martial law."

She stood and began to pace. "Domestic terror groups don't care about the law or people different than they are. We Asians know this only too well in America today. It would only take one dedicated extremist to use this stuff and cause widespread chaos, transforming protestors into killers."

Mac was taken aback by his friend's sudden change. "Where could this powder be manufactured?" he asked, hoping to calm her with questions of fact. "How hard would it be to make?"

"Any sophisticated pharmacological facility could do it," Grace replied. "Mac, I bet your monkeys were testing a compound that could destabilize an entire country. We could be facing world chaos if it were ever released."

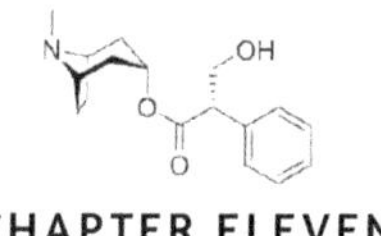

CHAPTER ELEVEN

THE RIO EXPERIMENT

RIO DE JANEIRO, BRAZIL
FEBRUARY 16, 2021

Hildo Avado looked down at the Carnival parade with pride and affection. Since his Rio de Janeiro childhood, he had attended almost every repetition of the Carnival celebration. His status had risen with time. In his childhood, he was relegated to the fringes of the crowd, pleading to sit on his father's shoulders to see. As he got older, he became involved with the parade itself and saw it from a participant's viewpoint. Now a revered Brazilian neurosurgeon, he watched from an elegant hotel room as a medical consultant to the parade committee.

This year the official parade had been canceled because of COVID-19, but boisterous Brazilians had insisted on having a celebration nonetheless. In response, all the usual police and other precautions had been ordered by the mayor of Rio.

Opening the large windows of his third-floor hotel room, Hildo closed his eyes and placed himself in the throngs below. The throbbing samba beat reverberated in the Sambadrome, punctuated with the cheers and songs of the scantily clad parade-goers. Bright costumes, raucous laughter, pulsing rhythm, mixed scents of flowers and perfume and sweat and caipirinhas; these brought again the memories of his youth.

February was always steaming hot in Rio. During Carnival, in the wild prelude to the weeks of Lenten discipline, excited people did crazy things. This was a signature celebration of Brazilian life, an ecstasy of religious, pagan, and multicultural traditions.

There were also kindnesses. In the street, plastic bottles of water were being distributed to paradegoers by a generous group. Much better than plastic necklaces from traditional floats. Hildo returned to his desk.

The sounds of alarms, shouting, and shattering glass brought him back to the window half an hour later. He looked down on the street scene in disbelief.

Where he had seen people dancing and singing, he now saw mayhem. Dozens of rioters filled the boulevard, attacking anyone in their way. Their shouts and their victims' screams filled the air. Smoke billowed from an open convertible sitting in the middle of the street, flames licking from its upholstery, windows smashed despite its open cockpit, tires slashed and trunk sprung open.

Store windows lay in shards on the sidewalk, and looters freely passed through them, grinning in triumph as they exited with armfuls of electronics and other goods. Their triumph was usually short-lived as others tore the loot out of their hands. A few shops which had boarded up their windows had been violated as well, some by dousing them in the sugar cane fuel used by cars and set on fire.

At the intersection below him, the mob had trapped several policemen, who disappeared under a sea of rioters. Several minutes later they crawled in pools of blood as the crowd moved on. Men, women, and children lay on the sidewalk, some trying to stop bleeding with their bare hands, some scrambling to any safe location they could find, a few with twisted bodies suggesting they would never move again.

Seeing the spectators injured on the street below, Avado's first instinct was to rush down to help. At the elevator, he realized how foolhardy this would be. Without protective gear and backup, he was certain to become one of the victims.

He returned to his room and called the mayor of Rio, the man who had appointed him to his position as neurosurgical consultant to Carnival.

The mayor preempted his question. "Hildo, I know why you're calling. I'm watching the mayhem from my balcony. We're mobilizing police and army troops. Stay in your hotel room. We'll take care of this."

Even three floors above the street, Avado felt the angry energy of the mob below him. They swept past and returned again, destroying anything in their way. Men threw fire extinguishers at each other. Flagpoles became clubs, and necklaces became tools for strangling. With the scanty costumes of Carnival, victims had no clothing to stem the bleeding from their wounds or to cover their abrasions.

The number of injured spectators increased. Riot police in combat gear, protected by Kevlar, helmets and crowd control shields, pushed back at the crowd without mercy. They battered and sprayed the rioters until one by one, the perpetrators were driven into corners and subdued. Miscreants were cuffed, disabled, and loaded into police wagons to be carted away.

Six hours after the rampage began, there were no rioters in the streets, although the storefronts and sidewalks still held the scars of the uprising. Blood stained the columns of buildings, and doors and windows were smashed.

Avado looked again at the streets and at the television coverage and shook his head as he went to bed.

The next morning, he learned that twenty people had died and over one hundred parade goers were in hospitals as victims of injuries inflicted by a festive gathering that erupted out of control. Most of the rioters were Brazilian citizens without any previous police records. Asked about why they had destroyed property and attacked other spectators at the event, they could give no reason. They said they became furious at annoyances they now saw as trivial.

Avado remained deeply troubled by what he had seen. As a neurosurgeon, he understood that human behavior is controlled by the brain. Something bizarre had happened to the perception and judgment of the rioters. He needed to understand what disconnect had led to such violence.

The experience of Carnival made Avado think of the newsfeeds of a mob attacking the United States Capitol in Washington on January sixth, 2021. He and his friends had watched this event with apprehension and amazement. He now wondered if the Rio disaster had the same dynamic.

He called his associate Duncan MacGregor, who co-chaired a World Federation of Neurosurgery committee with him, to ask his opinion about similarities and differences in the two events.

Avado summarized what he had witnessed the day before. "I want to know if the events here are similar to what happened at your Capitol."

"Show me what happened," Mac said. "You picked a great time to call. I still have an hour before I have to go into the hospital."

Avado remembered that Rio was just two hours ahead of Boston time despite the thousands of miles between the two cities. On a shared Zoom screen, he streamed videos he had taken from his hotel balcony. "To begin, here's the typical scene at the celebration. It's a huge party. Not exactly safe, but fundamentally friendly. Everyone knows to leave wallets and pocketbooks at home. Parade-goers care for each other. Look at these people. They are handing out bottled water. I won't bore you with more of normal Carnival. The real problem starts about half an hour after this."

He moved the time cursor forward and showed a few people beginning to push others around them. Those others pushed back, and individual fights broke out. As more spectators became involved, some attacking directly and others assisting their colleagues, the clusters of combatants grew.

The addition of weapons to the fighting upgraded the violence. Participants broke windows and used glass shards as weapons, stole knives, guns, and anything they could find from the shops they entered through broken doors and windows.

Escalation into murderous brutality took only a few minutes. Men and women slashed each other with glass, stabbed, bludgeoned, strangled. Half an hour after the beginning of the unrest, there was general mayhem.

"It doesn't look like there are any specific inciting events," Mac said.

"Would that make a difference?" Avado asked.

"All the difference in the world. Let me show you some recently released images from the Capitol uprising." He took over the screen to stream videos from a rally outside the White House just before the march on the Capitol. The then-president, several politicians, and other speakers exhorted the crowd to "take back their country," "kick ass," and engage in "trial by combat." A crowd marched down Pennsylvania Avenue to overpower an inadequate complement of Capitol Police.

Then Avado watched once again the breaching of the citadel of American democracy. White-skinned insurgents broke down doors, shattered windows, and scaled walls to gain entry. They beat police officers, urinated and defecated on the walls, took selfies in Congressional chairs and left threatening notes, even erected a gallows to hang the Vice-President.

Even though this was not his country, Avado felt angry, anxious, and betrayed. This should never happen in America.

Mac had not said anything so far. He interjected. "Superficially, the crowd looks the same as the Carnival partygoers. But watch carefully here."

Avado's breathing accelerated as he viewed the images now on the screen. Well-organized paramilitary clusters identified by their distinctive clothing, coalesced within the mob and led a charge toward the Senate and House chambers. They smashed windows and doors in the corridors with chairs, face shields, and fire extinguishers. Face-painted supporters with MAGA hats joined rioters in full military regalia. Some had zip ties of the kind used for tying up hostages.

"This is different than what I saw on the news," Avado said. "What you're showing me now looks like a well-organized coup attempt. We know about military takeovers in Brazil. Are you sure these clips aren't edited in some way?"

"Not manipulated at all except to run them together. And there's more," Mac continued. "Turn up your volume."

Avado could now distinguish the rioters communicating with bullhorns above the uncoordinated milling of the crowd. "There is a room on the other side of the door we can use to gather and co-ordinate," one voice said. Shouts of "We're here to kill the Speaker of the House," and "Hang the Vice President," and "this is our chamber, and we're taking it back," filled the air.

"The crowd targeted these politicians because the president and his cronies told it to," Mac explained.

"But I can't believe these videos," Avado said. "They are not at all how the event was presented on the world news. They make the January 6 insurrection look like a planned attack, not a spontaneous demonstration. I don't understand."

"That's the point," Mac said. "The Capitol uprising is completely different from what you saw in Rio. We had governmental officials, members of Congress, and domestic terrorists spurred on by the loser ex-president himself, combining to disrupt the electoral process." He stared into the camera. "I assume there are no similar Brazilian groups who would use Carnival to create such political chaos."

He turned back to the keyboard. "In case you don't believe me, here are videos showing just how pernicious the rhetoric before January 6 was."

Mac streamed excerpts from speeches extending back at least six years. They seemed increasingly comfortable with white supremacy, claimed that voting for anyone but the failed president and his cronies would be the end of the United States, and demonized all his political opponents.

"What do those comments have to do with the Capitol insurrection?" Avado asked. "They're just political propaganda."

"They have everything to do with it," Mac answered. "The Capitol riot was the product of months of preparation, a deliberate initiative to destroy the democratic system, to stoke fringe right-wing violent groups to overthrow an election."

"And the Rio riot?"

"Was a different kind of event entirely."

"It looks the same to me," Avado said.

"There may have been the same kind of anger and violence," Mac replied, "but the Capitol insurrection resulted from provocation by a political party and its leaders. Yours came out of the blue."

"Why was the Rio riot so violent, then?"

"I don't know," Mac said. "It's more violent than the storming of the Capitol."

"But isn't it *more* worrisome to have something like this happen without any apparent cause?"

"Yes," Mac said. "Can you possibly get a blood sample from a participant in the riot and send it to me frozen?"

"I can try. I assume you have a hypothesis about what caused this."

"I do, but it's so wild I'd rather wait before sharing it. Thanks in advance for any help you can give."

Mac hung up and called Jim Brogan, the CIA deputy director of intelligence who had dispatched him to Tangier.

"I think I have information that may be relevant to the Morocco monkey murder," Mac began.

"I'm glad someone has. Our investigation has gone nowhere. Whoever's involved knows how to hide a trail."

"No luck with facial recognition of the people beside the cage on the videos we saw?"

"The quality was too poor," Brogan answered. "What's your new information?"

"A friend in Rio de Janeiro just called me about violence erupting during the Carnival parade there. Twenty people died and hundreds were hospitalized. It seemed to affect a small group, and the rioters involved don't have any idea what set them off."

"Just like the macaques."

"And just before the rampage, a group passed out water bottles."

"You think the water could carry the Berserker compound? Isn't it more likely that the spectators involved were just more drunk than usual?"

"This was no drunken crowd, Jim. It was normal citizens, people who had no history of misbehavior. Rio has no problem dealing with excessive alcohol intake at Carnival, but the police said they had never seen such a violent group. Can you review the videos of the parade to track down the water bottle company?"

"Should be easy. I'll get back to you."

Mac's next call went to Grace Wu.

"Grace, we have a situation that might involve the Berserker compound."

"You mean the Rio Carnival massacre?"

"How did you know?"

"BBC world news. Are you sure it wasn't just too many caipirinhas? Alcohol is still the number one drug that produces violent behavior."

"This was no drunken crowd," Mac said. "Rio has dealt with intoxicated and drugged-up paradegoers for years. This was something far more sinister." Mac said.

"What kind of violence are you talking about?"

"People mauling each other and destroying property without provocation."

"Words also seem to be able to achieve that goal. Remember the president and his lawyer talking just before the Capitol siege?"

"Nothing like that happened here. I think the Berserker drug removed the need for words—that ingestion could set off a mob. I've asked a friend to send blood from one of the aggressors. Could you analyze it for Berserker compound?"

"Of course. I hope I find nothing."

A very different discussion took place in the Morlock executive suite in New York only a few hours after the end of the Carnival episode. Rufus Morlock and Steve Therman reviewed a video sent to them by a Rio operative.

"Splendid," Morlock exclaimed as he watched the celebration morph from joyous to deadly. "This compound certainly works. With it, we can create chaos in demonstrations around the country."

"Except for two things," Therman said. "First, we don't know what contribution alcohol makes to this situation. We need to show that the compound works on people who aren't already high on alcohol and other drugs."

Morlock tapped his fingers.

"And second," Therman continued, "we don't have enough of the stuff to use for any widespread demonstrations since our production facility was destroyed. We're manufacturing more, but the earliest we would have sufficient drug is the end of June."

"We don't need the compound yet," Morlock said. "It'll take a couple of months to get our people around the world ready to go. Just be sure we have the Rio videos to show our international patriots in Boston next week."

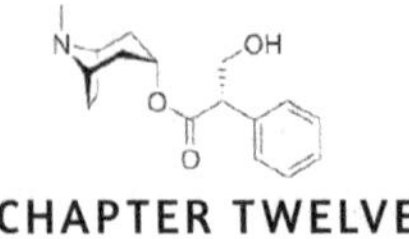

CHAPTER TWELVE

THE BOSTON FISH EXCHANGE

"Why do we have to go to the Boston office for this Zoom meeting?" Lorcan Morlock asked his father as they boarded the helicopter on the roof of their Manhattan building. "And how come so early?"

Morlock senior tried to suppress his annoyance. Seven a.m. was not early for him. "Our Right TV, Wall St. Times, and Stock Exchange offices belong in our Sixth Avenue building. Our international patriotic efforts are best carried out somewhere else." Why was his fifty-year old son so dense about these matters? Although Morlock tried to avoid direct confrontation because Lorcan would have to continue the work, he sometimes felt like throttling his son and heir.

Morlock turned his head to watch early dawn spread over Central Park. The ride was amazingly smooth—the Eurocopter was the quietest and most comfortable chopper in the world. And it was fast, taking less than an hour to get to Boston.

After they passed over their estate on the north fork of Long Island, Rufus Morlock spoke again. "And to continue our discussion about why Boston, it's a great place to start a revolution. History repeating itself."

"Just remember my discovery started the whole Berserker drug business," Lorcan said with a frown almost becoming a pout.

"Really? How so?" his father asked.

"I tracked down the Lindisfarne bible and bought it from the monks. I had the idea of cutting open the thick cover to find the hidden page that showed the orb and the powder. You wouldn't know about Berserker without me."

"If I hadn't put you on the search," the old man said, annoyed at his son's claim, "you wouldn't have discovered anything. I'm the collector. I was the one looking for medieval bibles. And after you pulled out the vellum picture, I was the one who realized what the orb and powder meant."

He paused. His dense son still appeared unconvinced. "And Therman found the actual orb and powder in a God-forsaken English church, had it analyzed, and arranged for chemical modification to make it more effective. It was also Therman who set up the manufacturing plant for our modern Berserker drug. You're an infinitesimal speck of the story."

Morlock senior lapsed into silence. Did he have to depend on this privileged dilettante son to carry on his work? Would Steve Therman, who had contributed so much including the event about to unfold, be a worthier heir?

In two hours, patriot groups from thirty countries would hear about the Berserker compound Morlock had replicated from the sample in the Lindisfarne orb. It could change innocent demonstrators into murderous mobs and destabilize entire countries. The need for a clandestine base such as the Boston Fish Exchange office to carry out this social disruption was obvious. Why was his son so stupid?

"This is a big morning, Lorcan," Morlock said as Boston came into view. "Therman has arranged for representatives of international organizations from ISIS to the IRA to learn about our Berserker powder. Today our work changes from propaganda to action."

The rotor blades slowed and whirred to a stop on a helipad sitting at the end of the fish pier. Behind them was Boston's inner harbor. On the other side of the building, warehouses lined the long passage to Seaport Boulevard.

A wintry wind blustered off the Atlantic, bringing fresh sea air with its chill. A gray sky carried the possibility of snow. The cries of seagulls diving to snatch fish from the sea mixed with the intermittent rumble of airplanes taking off and landing at Logan Airport.

Two security guards greeted father and son after they stepped off the Eurocopter and opened the door into a vaulted rotunda thirty feet in diameter. Floor-to-ceiling windows of this round room provided a spectacular view of Boston Harbor. A partition blocked off the back half of the room. An oversized desk and leather chair provided the only seating in the front half of the space. Large video monitors stretched along the front wall, and a video camera focused on the chair. From it, Morlock could see all the monitors at once.

"Lorcan, get behind the wall with the technician," Morlock said. "You can observe from there. Maybe someday you'll be able to arrange what I'm about to pull off."

With the look of a whipped dog, Lorcan slunk around the partition as a young man in jeans and sneakers appeared. "I think we're all set, Mr. M," the technician said. "You can watch the participants on the monitors. They won't see you directly, however. Your avatar will speak to them with an electronically altered voice."

Morlock loved this high-ceilinged circular room that was once a Fish Exchange. Sitting in it was like having an office right beside the sea. Bewitched by the ocean since his New Zealand childhood, he sometimes imagined he could smell cod and bluefish while he sat at his desk manipulating the world.

Modelling itself on the British Empire at its height, his media empire would restore the cult of the strong leader. Social chaos caused by the Berserker compound would foment the rise of autocrats. The democracies of the world would perish, and business oligarchs would come into their own. The British Empire relied on dominance of the sea to create its political domain. Morlock used airwave dominance to develop his media domain, but soon he would add political disruption to his toolkit.

Blackout curtains slid along the windows and doors as the monitors flashed to life. A spotlight illuminated Morlock as he began to speak from his seat behind the desk. On the screens he heard his voice, electronically altered, emitted from the mouth of a blond, blue-eyed, six-foot-six male. "Great avatar," Morlock said. "Truly Nordic. And I look thirty years younger. You technical folks have done a great job."

He rehearsed the lines he was about to say to the gathering. "You men represent the world's last hope. As dedicated patriots in your own countries, you realize that your governments have failed your people. I have created a weap-on to allow you to prevail in your fight against tyranny."

"We're ready, Mr. M.," the technician called. Morlock waited for the large monitors to show the attendees as they signed in.

Instead, the monitors went black.

When they lit again, Steven Therman's face filled all the screens.

"Hello, Rufus," Therman's larger-than-life visage said.

"What the hell is this?" Morlock shouted, standing in his position behind the desk. "Where are you streaming from?"

"A safe place. And we've changed the plan," Therman's image said.

"Lorcan, get out here," Morlock called. He could feel his pulse rise.

Morlock's son stepped out from behind the partition, made a gesture of apology, and said "I think you should hear Steve out. I'm on his side. Why don't you sit down and listen for a change?"

Morlock was furious, but another emotion boiled within him at the same time. His spineless prep school son was showing some grit.

He sat.

"I knew you would never listen to reason," Therman continued, "so Lorcan and I decided to abort your plan. And by the way, don't think the guards will save you. They and the technicians are on board with us."

Morlock looked at the partition, where Lorcan and the other people who had been behind the screen now stood with their attention directed at the monitors.

Therman continued. "Here's the deal. You're on the wrong track. The Berserker powder should be used in the USA before international groups get their hands on it. America first, last and always. The Zoom meeting you tried to arrange with groups from around the world was the last straw. I never set it up. You can't trust Arabs and Russians and Chinese. Hell, you can't even trust your own kind. We need to destabilize our own country, get the right leadership in place, and then think about toppling other governments."

"And how would you do that, smartass?" Morlock said. He began to imagine ways to have Therman eliminated.

"I've already cultivated dozens of American patriot organizations willing to restore America to its greatness," Therman said. "Our former president disappointed and betrayed them. He was a narcissistic psychopath, a person who always used other people for his purposes, a pathological liar. His followers are ready for a change. Unlike him, I won't leave them high and dry. What I promise, I deliver."

"And you'll want to be the boss?"

"Hell no. I'm too smart for that. But I will be the king-maker behind the scenes. With Lorcan to help, of course." On screen, Therman looked beyond Morlock to the partition where Lorcan gave him a thumbs up.

"You'd give the powder away to any American patriot group who wants it?" Morlock asked.

"No. Fifty groups, and each one will have to show they can arrange demonstrations to destabilize local governments. They must all buy into the idea of making this a country run by white men for white men." He stared Morlock in the face. "Isn't that what you wanted all along?"

"Not the way you're describing."

"Right. You wanted to take over the minds of the American people with your media empire. That's inefficient and uncertain and takes too long."

"So you would..." *Where was the bastard broadcasting from?*

"Give each of the fifty groups a cash donation and a few kilos of Berserker powder," Therman said.

"How do you know their plans will work?" Morlock played for time as he decided on his next move.

"Require proposals and a track record."

"Why should I trust anything you say?"

"You shouldn't, but if you don't you will live in fear every minute for the rest of your life. You can eliminate me, but I know your habits and weakness better than anyone, and I have a network of friends who don't share my scruples. Who will be your assassin? Your chauffeur? Your bodyguard? Maybe even your own heir when he gets tired of waiting."

Morlock felt apoplectic. He had welcomed Steven Therman into his circle as an assistant, and over the years the bastard had recruited Lorcan to his cause. Morlock would let them try their scheme, since it did not preclude his own plan later, but one mistake—

"And there's one other thing," Therman said. "My patriot groups will want proof that our stuff works in a crowd of normal citizens. The Rio experiment was not enough— everyone there was probably stoned or drunk. We'll have to arrange for another demonstration."

Morlock immediately understood how to remain dominant. He would go along with Therman's modification of his global plan, could consider the American phase the first experiments. But to divide and conquer, Morlock would put Lorcan in charge of the project. If Lorcan and Therman achieved the desired results, good for them. If they didn't, he would neuter them the way he'd cut down so many other rivals on his way to power.

Therman continued, apparently unaware of the direction of Morlock's thought. "I've already told them we would do something in France. We have to wait five weeks for enough new drug to be manufactured and bottled. April in Paris should be a perfect place to do our final human experiment."

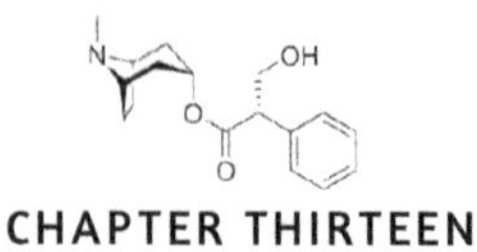

CHAPTER THIRTEEN

PYRAMID 03041400

In his years of neurosurgical practice, Mac had learned to answer calls at any hour of the night. When the phone rang at six a.m., his brain flashed from sleep to alertness.

"Mac, you said I should call right away if I found something significant." Grace Wu's voice. He moved with his cell phone away from the bed to the living room.

Grace continued. "I was tracking down possible manufacturers of this new Berserker drug and came across a company called Amygdalin. I couldn't get access to their backroom data, so I asked a friend to "look into" it for me. Full disclosure: he hacked into their site."

"And?" Mac remembered the name from Tangier.

"The first thing he found was a message sent a few minutes ago. It went to a scrambled email list. I'm not sure what it means, but it looks weird enough to me to be important."

"I'm all ears," Mac said. He wrote down what Grace said next, then repeated it back to her. *P-y-r-a-m-i-d- 0-3-0-4-1-4-0-0. There you'll see what you've been waiting for.* "That's all there is?" he asked. "What do you think it means?"

"No idea," Grace said. "I don't know anything about the

numbering of pyramids—I thought you might have run into something in your travels. Could this be a tag for a particular archeological site in Egypt? But how would that have anything to do with Berserker?"

"Maybe that's their new manufacturing facility or storehouse. One of my buddies from residency is both a surgeon and amateur Egyptologist. I'm going to call him to ask."

"At 6:15 a.m.?"

"This was important enough for you to wake me. He's probably up already."

"I hope he's a good friend."

"Used to be. We stayed up all night together on trauma call during our training."

Dr. Piers Chaplin was not as understanding as Mac thought. "You want to know what?" Chaplin said, sounding as if he were still asleep. "May I remind you it is 6:15 in the morning?"

"Is there a numbering system for pyramids that would make sense of the sequence Pyramid 03041400?"

"Why do you want to know this so urgently?" Chaplin asked.

"Some research I'm tracking down."

"So before dawn has cracked, you call me, wake my wife and the dog, and ask me a question that could wait until tomorrow, or maybe until next year? I've got a full patient schedule this morning."

"I wouldn't call if it weren't important." Mac thought perhaps it would have been better to contact the Museum of Fine Arts Egyptology department.

"Important is in the mind of the thinker," Chaplin said. "But to answer your question, there is no pyramid numbering system that would make sense of your sequence. I expect 1400 means 1400 hours. The Egyptians use the twenty-four-hour clock. Great to talk with you."

Mac listened to the buzz of the dial tone for a few seconds and realized his colleague had hung up. "Thanks, Piers," he said as he tapped his phone off.

He called Grace back. "That's not a number for pyramid identification. My archeological friend did suggest that 1400 might mean two p.m. If that's true, maybe 0304 is March 4."

"Egyptians put the day before the month, so 0304 is April 3."

"Five days from today." Mac's heart skipped a beat. Was Egypt the country where he could find out the secrets of the drug he was seeking?

At breakfast later that morning, Mac introduced as innocently as he could the possibility of a quick excursion to Egypt. Lauren almost dropped her coffee cup, Maggie stopped licking cream cheese from her bagel, and Peter froze in mid-bite with egg hanging out of his sandwich.

"This is not a time to be travelling to that part of the world," Lauren said. "Why would you even think of going there?"

"My friend Grace Wu—" he was interrupted by an incoming call. "Grace?" he answered.

"I was looking at the message again," Grace said. "I wanted to be sure you copied it down right. Pyramid has an *e* at the end. Must be a French source."

Mac added the *e*, making the message "Pyramide 03041400."

"By the way," Grace continued, "I haven't gotten any specimens from Rio to analyze. Any luck with that?"

"Not yet," Mac said, and turned back to his family as the call disconnected.

Lauren repeated her question "Why Egypt?" Mac started to explain, then decided he would just show them the piece of paper with the code on it. "A friend of mine intercepted this message," he said, "and we believe it contains information about a secret meeting."

"I think the numbers mean March fourth at two p.m." Peter said.

"Unless you're in Europe or the UK, where it would mean April 3 at two p.m." Lauren added, joining the discussion. "And I'll bet this *Pyramide*—she made air quotes—has nothing to do with Egypt."

She fumbled with her cell phone and brought it over to Mac with an image on its screen.

Of course. His head injury must have rendered him stupid. The Pyramide was no Egyptian antiquity. It was the I.M. Pei entrance to the Louvre. He had visited it several times. It took his family to perceive the obvious.

After Lauren and the children began school, Mac called Jim Brogan to ask whether there was any unusual activity of known American terrorists travelling to Paris.

"Weird that you should ask," Brogan said. "We've noted a dozen group leaders leaving for Paris around the second of April. We're monitoring closely."

"What about Cairo?" Mac asked.

"Cairo is always turbulent, but nothing new."

Mac described the note Grace Wu had intercepted.

"Mac, this might be a really big deal," Brogan said with a voice trembling with excitement. "Can you to go to Paris? I don't have anyone else available on short notice, and I don't want to bother the French authorities without stronger proof that something bad is happening. A dozen itineraries doesn't add up to a terrorist plot."

"But you're worried," Mac said.

"Aren't you? I'm particularly concerned that the whole affair may have something to do with our Moroccan monkeys. No one else understands this as well as you. Whatever's going to happen in Paris on April 3 may be a further test of the Berserker drug."

"I think I could arrange coverage for a couple of days." Mac said. "Could I invite Amara Zadi to assist? I need a trusted ally, and she knows everything about the monkeys."

"Fine from my point of view."

Mac called Amara and asked whether she would be interested in a visit to Paris to follow up the Moroccan monkey story. She enthusiastically agreed to join and seemed offended that he refused to stay at the family condominium there.

On evening of April second, Mac boarded a direct flight to the city of light. His family, ensnared by school projects, stayed in Boston despite Maggie's entreaties to join him.

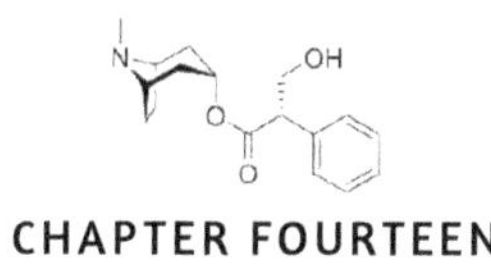

THE LOUVRE

PARIS, FRANCE
APRIL 3, 2021

Mac arrived in Paris after a sleepless night. His flight plus hours in immigration, COVID testing, and customs left him exhausted as he exited from the terminal.

His spirits improved when he saw a masked Amara Zadi waving from the other side of the street. She looked quintessentially French in black turtleneck, jeans, mask, and amethyst necklace. "I have a limo for us," she said as they elbow bumped.

In two minutes, they were on their way to their rendezvous with the Louvre. They had an hour to make the two p.m. deadline. At the Carrousel Bridge that crossed the Seine to the museum, a solid line of cars stopped them.

"Today marks the reopening of the Louvre after a year of COVID-19 closure," Amara said in explanation. "Let's walk the rest of the way." She spoke to the chauffeur in rapid-fire Arabic, slipped him a fifty Euro note, and started across the bridge on foot.

Mac kept up easily with her brisk pace, resisting the urge to stop and admire the *bateaux-mouches* and other boats on the Seine. Spring foliage adorned the trees and the sun shone with unusual April intensity. He had difficulty imagining that this quiet scene might soon be the site of a terrorist demonstration.

Once they reached the plaza, the object of their quest glittered like a diamond in the afternoon sun. Homage to the pyramids in Egypt, the glass and steel Pyramide du Louvre erupted from the center of the French Renaissance buildings around it like an artifact from a future world.

The plaza between them and the Louvre was packed. Mac directed Amara to the Arc de Triomphe du Carrousel, at the far edge of the plaza. "We can observe from here," he said. "And we'll be out of the way."

The scene was a model of crowd control. Hundreds of hopefuls lined up to be the first visitors to enter the Louvre, shuttered for months during the pandemic. Men and women of every color stood in line; some of them munched on sandwiches, most of them played with their smartphones. Vendors hawked coffee and croissants. People from one wagon seemed to be giving out free bottles of water. Gendarmes supervised, but seemed to enjoy the brisk April morning as much as the tourists.

"I want to check the crowd for familiar faces," Amara said, heading toward the line of visitors waiting at the Pyramide.

"Be careful. Don't drink any bottled water," Mac shouted, but she had already moved out of earshot.

She returned carrying two containers of water, one already opened. "There must be two hundred people in that line. We may have a long afternoon. I brought you some water."

"Where did you get that?" Mac asked, his voice uneasy. He noted that the logo on the free water bottles was the same as the brand Avado had mentioned during Carnival.

"A guy was handing the bottles out," she said, then became very silent.

"Water," she said.

"Exactly," Mac said, expecting she had just made the connection with the powdered water given to the monkeys in the Tangier videos. "I'll take those bottles for analysis."

Amara handed them over and added, "I only had two swallows. I'm going back to find the vendor."

"I'd rather you stay here," Mac shouted, but she was gone.

Twenty minutes later she returned. "When the water bottle guy saw me heading toward him, he ran off with his cart. Still had about sixty bottles on it."

She approached Mac to put her chin within inches of his. "But I'm bothered by your insinuation I should not have taken any of the water. You shouldn't criticize me." Her tone seemed completely out of character.

Mac was taken aback by her aggressive stance. "I apologize if I offended you. I didn't mean it. I'm just worried about what might be in the bottle."

"Sorry's not enough," she said. "You don't know what it's like to be demeaned and criticized in everything you do." She stared at him with blazing eyes and clenched fists.

"Amara, I think you may have taken some of the Berserker drug in that water."

"Sure, criticize me again." She strode toward him.

A giant whose shaved head towered above the rest of the

crowd finished a bottle of water and pushed forward in the line waiting to enter. "Look over there," Mac said, trying to distract her. "I think some other people are feeling the same effects you are," Mac said, and began to move toward the man.

An elderly woman tripped Mac with an umbrella. Several people waiting elbowed others and picked fights. Gendarmes raced to block them, but found their batons appropriated by the crowd.

As Mac crossed the plaza, the quiet scene evolved into an uproar. Shouts and accusations filled the air, and the orderly line broke into dozens of clustered antagonists. A few people slashed at each other or tried to defend themselves.

Mac thought back to Hildo's description of Carnival. Was this a repeat of the chaos of that event? He was convinced the water bottles had the Berserker compound in them, that he was seeing the effects of the drug. Fortunately, only a few people seem to have gotten bottles.

Mac could hear the giant's heavily accented shouts in a language he did not recognize. The tourists in front of him turned back and began to protest. As they tried to block him, he became more and more agitated at their opposition.

"I'm going to stop him," Amara said.

"What are you talking about? He's twice as big as you are," Mac said, grabbing her arm.

"No matter," she tore away and began running toward the giant.

He turned as she approached and swatted her as if she were a fly.

She fell to the ground. Mac rushed to her side, ignoring the curses and kicks of the crowd who collided with him. In the few seconds it took him to reach her, she had curled up in a protective ball to shield her head and face from the mob.

He checked her quickly. Facial contusions, a few abrasions. No evidence of broken bones or concussion. He thanked his lucky stars she had taken only a few sips of the tainted water.

He helped her back to the arch, buffeted by the pushing and shoving of bystanders. At his destination, he maneuvered a disposable poncho from his pocket and spread it on the ground for her to lie on.

"You OK now?" he asked as she slumped against the arch.

"Yes, thanks to you," she said through lips swollen and bruised. "It was the water, wasn't it? That's what set this off. Now I know how the compound makes its victims feel. I thought I could take on anyone and felt furious at anyone who got in the way. Including you!"

The giant continued toward the Pyramide, dragging half a dozen people with him. The crowd turned on him and each other. Some seemed particularly aggressive, presumably the people who drank the most water. Men attacked other men with bare hands. Women pounded the faces of their opponents with the heels of their shoes. One elderly woman thrust a knitting needle into an assailant's chest as he attacked her. Teenagers kicked, head-butted, and twisted.

The giant reached the head of the line, guzzling water from the bottle. If people got in his way, he swung them around to clear his path, shouting epithets, spitting and spraying sweat like Godzilla's brother. He ran toward the structure full tilt. Moving head down with increasing velocity, he became a three-hundred-pound human projectile.

He crashed through an entire panel of the glass and wire structure and disappeared.

Mac and Amara raced to the gaping hole left by his entrance. On the floor thirty feet below, the man lay spread-eagled on the reception area of the Louvre, immobile in a pool of blood. Cables shorn by the force of his attack swung in the April breeze.

After ten minutes EMT's arrived, did a quick examination, and shook their heads. They did not attempt resuscitation but loaded the bald giant onto a stretcher and transported him away.

On the plaza, the arrival of dozens of police brought the situation under control. A few bystanders attacked the gendarmes with flowerpots and tree branches, but the chief attackers were isolated and put in police wagons.

"I need to examine that man's brain," Mac said to Amara as the giant's body exited.

"How will you arrange that?" Amara asked.

"It may be possible." Mac called Jim Brogan, who picked up on the first ring. "You OK?" Brogan asked. "My people tell me all hell has broken loose around the Louvre. Thanks to your intel, we could convince the French police to have extra troops ready, but it sounds like a real bad show."

"I have a favor to ask," Mac said.

"Before you ask it, did Amara Zadi join you? Is she OK?" Brogan asked. "I don't want to make this an international incident."

"Yes, she helped and is fine," Mac said.

"Great. What's the favor?"

"Can you get me permission to do an autopsy?"

"Where?"

"The Pitie-Saltpetriere Hospital."

"Anyone in particular?"

"A massive muscle man who just dove head-first into the Pyramide. I want to see if he had the same changes in his amygdala the monkeys in Tangier showed."

"I think I can do that. Give me thirty minutes."

Mac and Amara hailed a cab on the Quai Francois Mitterand, crossed the Pont des Arts to the Left Bank, joined the crawling traffic of the Quais de Conti, des Grands Augustins, and Saint-Michel, then wound through back streets to the Boulevard St. Michel. They arrived at the Mazarin gate of the Hopital Universitaire de la Pitie-Salpetriere within twenty minutes.

A masked woman greeted them at the door. Under her watchful eye, they put on gowns, gloves, caps, and masks and followed to the autopsy suite. Three gleaming stainless-steel tables lay in the center of the room, with spotlights and a set of saws, chisels, knives, and other tools beside each table. The floor sloped to the center with a drain for blood and other body fluids. Coffin-sized slots with tags to mark each corpse lay against one wall.

"It is highly unusual to let a doctor from America do even part of an autopsy here. You must have a lot of political clout. Of course, you know you can only examine the brain. Your man is on Table three," the attendant said in good English, and left.

Walking over to the designated autopsy table, Mac turned the giant's head and marked out an incision that resembled a question mark in front of the left ear. He incised the skin and muscle, held the soft tissue flap off the bone with a retractor, and drilled a hole in the bone. He sawed through the skull and lifted a bone flap, showing the firm dural lining of the brain. Scissors opened that, and with a suction apparatus he opened into the left lateral ventricle.

"Yes! Look at that amygdala, Amara," he exclaimed as he exposed a bloody structure the size of a baseball in the depths of the exposure. "That's all I needed to see. The amygdala is supposed to be the size of an almond, but it has had major swelling and bleeding." He took blood and brain specimens for later examination.

"I would say something has exploded," Amara said as she peered into the cavity.

"Good description," Mac said. "My colleague Grace Wu says this happens in people who lack the enzyme to metabolize the Berserker drug. The compound's effects build up in them and cause the blood vessels to rupture. This giant's amygdala self-destructed, causing increased brain pressure and death."

"Definitely Berserker at work?" Amara asked.

"Yes. The giant must have swallowed a couple of bottles and felt the effects fast. This man and the monkey we saw in Tangier had the same brain changes and exhibited the same ultra-violent behavior. We're dealing with a compound that could destroy a government if it got into the wrong hands."

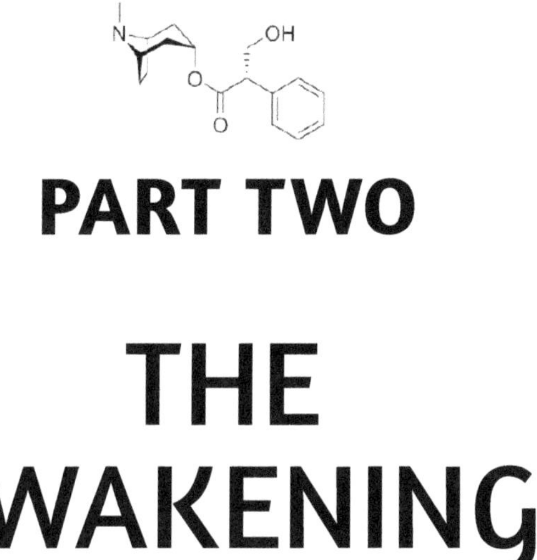

PART TWO

THE AWAKENING

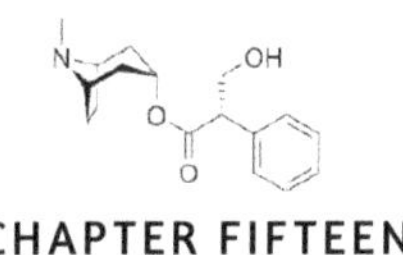

CHAPTER FIFTEEN

THERMAN AND MORLOCK JR.

MANHATTAN, NY
APRIL 4, 2021

"The Paris demonstration went well," Therman reported to Lorcan Morlock as he stood in front of the mahogany desk waiting to sit. He hated the Morlock penthouse in New York but had no choice in venue. "Ten of our patriot leaders were on the Louvre grounds when the riots broke out. They saw firsthand what the drug could do to a normal crowd."

"But we almost got busted," Lorcan said. "How did the police close it down so quickly? Did they have some kind of warning? And who was that woman who ran after our bottled water distributor?"

"I'm working on that," Therman said. For the first time, he felt unsure about his ability to swim in the waters he found himself in. Most of his life had been spent as a radio talk show host, where he could say whatever he wanted without consequence. Creating the Berserker production laboratories for Morlock senior had been a challenge which he had met by bribing other people to do it. Now he had to create a revolution and deal with Morlock's heir apparent, tasks that did not make him happy.

"Remember that since our Boston confrontation, my father put me in charge of you," Lorcan said, keeping Therman standing. "We hadn't worked out all the details when we pushed our plan for America first. Today I have to fix that. I need to know everything."

"Like what?" Therman was increasingly annoyed with this whelp.

"Will you be ready for July fourth?"

"Will *I* be ready? I thought we were doing this together," Therman said. "But yes, July fourth will be the day we create The Storm."

"But how are you going to do it exactly?"

"First, we get a handful of politicians on board. We've already bought a few members of the House and Senate to support what we're doing. Some of them helped to plan the January sixth insurrection, and we can use that as leverage. We should be able to get them on board for this project easily."

"How will you buy them?" Lorcan asked.

"I can't believe you're so naïve as to ask that question. The same way influence has always worked. Harassment, bribes, greed, fear. We already have several legislators in our pocket, and the party leadership encourages them to join us."

"What else?" Lorcan continued in attack mode.

"Second, we'll increase the misinformation we're spreading. Your Right TV network has already stopped COVID vaccination in its tracks. Personally, I don't know how you can stand looking at the deaths you caused, but that's on your conscience, not mine."

"Doesn't bother me a bit," Lorcan said. "Freedom of choice and all that bullshit."

"Selling Berserker should be easy in comparison," Therman said. "We'll argue that America is being taken over by Blacks and Hispanics and Asians, and the only solution is complete chaos followed by the emergence of a strong white Christian leader." Therman felt comfortable here. Misinformation was his world.

"So you'll use lies to cover what you're doing," Lorcan said. "We've talked about that—it's what our whole network is about. But give me specifics about the mechanism of disruption."

"A series of violent demonstrations all over the country, just as we've discussed before."

"But the details. How will you arrange the demonstrations?"

"Any excuse for a gathering. We'll hand out bottled water laced with the Berserker powder, just like we did in Rio and Paris. Doesn't matter what the original issue was to create a demonstration. All the protests will turn violent."

"How will you get a coordinated attack?'

"Use patriot groups already existing in the United States, like the Oath Takers and Proud Men. I already have dozens of these militia groups on board, and there are many hundred more in our fair country. We'll give fifty of them money and Berserker powder. For distribution and orders we'll be just like the church, with dioceses and parishes and all that."

"How, exactly?"

"Recruit dozens of patriot groups. There are more than eight hundred listed in our fair country. We'll give fifty of them money and Berserker powder. We'll have a distribution network like the church, with dioceses and parishes and all that."

"How many bishops? How many priests?"

Therman had never been held accountable for the bizarre plans he had touted to change the face of America. He considered himself a kind of twenty-first century Socrates, a horse fly stinging the establishment. He never thought he might have to create a blueprint for the actual change he proposed.

"We'll have fifty groups, picked geographically," he said, the assurance in his voice belying the queasiness in his stomach. *How could he be expected to be both brilliant and effective at the same time? How in hell am I going to choose the final fifty?*

"Do you have the groups picked?" Lorcan pressed, seeming to read Therman's mind.

"I'm working on that now," Therman lied. He felt like strangling Lorcan. He had bullied his way into a world of hard action he had never faced before. Thinking back on the January sixth insurrection at the Capitol and the words of the president's lawyer, he blurted out. "We'll have trial by combat."

Lorcan's head jerked up. He seemed to be paying attention now.

"Trial by combat?"

"Yes. I'll ask competing groups to carry out a specific task. The groups that succeed will be given the money."

"And what happens after the chaos the Berserker powder produces?" Lorcan asked.

"I don't have to tell you there are militia groups in most states waiting to take over control once the system is destabilized. Our job is to give them an excuse. They'll take care of the rest."

Lorcan nodded. "My father would approve of that method. You have two weeks to tell me who you have chosen. Get out. And in case you think you're the big shot now," Lorcan shouted as Therman got to the door, "remember that Morlock blood is thicker than the piss you represent in our organization."

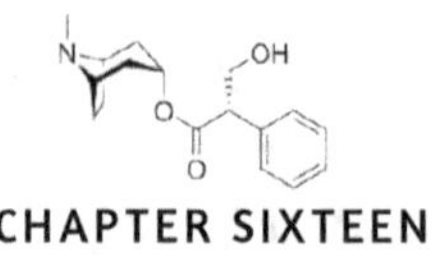

CHAPTER SIXTEEN

HAMMER

Congresswoman Sharon Hammer finished destroying her target's heart with ten slugs from her Glock 17, then put one bullet through its head for good measure.

GOOD SHOOTING, the sign flashed as the shredded outline was replaced by a fresh tracing. The lane set up for the next marksman.

The Virginia shooting range was a delight of sound and smoke for Hammer, taking her back to happy days in Texas. She removed the goggles and ear protectors, inhaled deeply, and invited the young man beside her to step up. "Ever shot a pistol before, Cabot? Or did they keep you chained to your desk at accounting school?"

She loved taunting young professionals who applied for her newly posted accounting job and thought they were so smart. It was worth the interviews to watch them slink away after they tried to match her shooting skill. And this guy looked like the nerdiest of them all, clean-shaven, thin, lacking any real muscle.

"A little," he said. With a casual glance at the target, he proceeded to decimate the heart and head in two clusters of perfectly executed shots.

"Were you always a smartass?" she shouted with a smile. "I have to say you're the first job candidate even to come close to a target cluster. Let's see how good you really are. Get your shots as close to mine as you can."

She aimed for the left eye of the newly positioned cardboard target and pulled the trigger. It entered exactly midpoint of the eye. Without much preparation, Cabot lifted and fired.

"Ha. You missed the whole damn board," Hammer said.

Cabot shrugged, took off his ear protectors and shouted, "Look more closely."

As she strained her vision, she realized his bullet entered exactly on top of hers. She tried three more, with the same result. "I think it's time for a beer," she said, checking to be sure it was after five o'clock. "I assume you drink. Consider it our second interview."

They crossed the street to the bar made up to resemble a Texas saloon. Seated with a bucket of Bud in front of her, she could begin the serious questioning.

"I'm not even going to ask where you learned to shoot like that. I'm going to start with QAnon. I assume you know what that is." She tipped back her first beer. That cold flash just put her in the mood she needed to discuss the sensitive position she was offering. And it had only come up when the guy from Winthrop Massachusetts, wherever the hell that was, called her to make a proposition.

Cabot nodded. "I've heard you called the Queen of QAnon."

"We still don't know who the real Q of QAnon is—no one does. But whoever it was, she figured out the real way things are. There's a deep state that controls us, a hidden government you don't see—rich businessmen, actors and producers from the entertainment industry, and of course Democratic politicians. They're out to kill our unborn babies, take away our guns, and create a new world order, a fascist police state. They even have secret ceremonies where they sacrifice children and eat them."

She saw the doubting look Cabot gave her. "You Northeast people are part of the problem. My Texas district is full of believers like me," Hammer continued. She wagged her finger at Cabot. "You may wonder how a grown woman, thirty-three with two children, could believe in a cult that includes sex trafficking, cannibalism, and Satan worship."

Cabot said nothing.

Hammer started on her second bottle. "Have you considered how it is that so many of the socialist policies we are adopting in our government continue to be pushed forward no matter who the president is? And take this most recent farce we called an election. I know for sure that dead people and illegal immigrants voted, that some votes were dumped in the river, and that those left-wing liberals like that Georgia Black woman completely rigged our system. The whole thing was a joke."

She slammed the empty beer bottle on the table. "Anyway, we have a chance to make this all stop. There's a guy who's planning to help us create the sort of unrest we will need to install a strong leader. Number 45 was the only president in the last century who has really understood the deep state and tried to block it, but he's a psychopath. We need somebody who can bring his agenda forward but doesn't have his psychiatric problems. And the first step is to create chaos."

"What's the real job you have in mind?" Cabot asked.

"The guy I'm in touch with will give us money, a lot of money, and some other stuff I can't describe right now. He's an answer to my prayers, but I need a way of making the funds untraceable. That also goes for other donors I don't want to be made public. Can't tell you where they're from, but they're crucial to my success in Washington. I don't want them to be tracked down."

"They're based in Moscow, I assume," Cabot said.

Hammer looked at him narrowed eyes. "Why would you say that?"

Cabot stared at her. "You think because I have a New England name and wear horn-rimmed glasses I'm stupid? I know who you are. I know Congress may throw you out because you're such a crude bitch. I know all that keeps you politically alive is the money you can raise. It doesn't surprise me that most of the funds can be traced to Russia, and that you want to launder it."

Hammer looked around the bar. "Will you shut up? God knows who might be listening right now."

Cabot started to rise. "I'll be going now."

"The hell you will," Hammer said. "You're just the man I've been looking for. You're hired."

And with that, Hammer felt herself giving into a new political world-- absolute obedience to the leader, support for patriot groups, guns at any cost, and of course a whole lot of foreign money to fund it all.

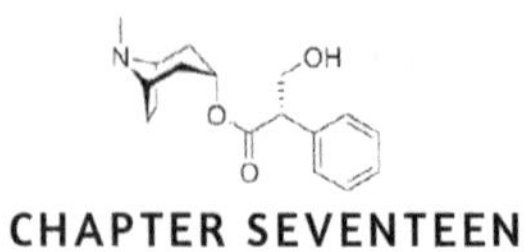

CHAPTER SEVENTEEN

THERMAN MEETS JANE

WINTHROP, MA
APRIL 16, 2021

Therman had a secret hideaway, a family summer home in Winthrop, Massachusetts. Held in his sister's married name, it was not easily traceable to him. It lay fallow and unclaimed for a year after his sister's death. At the beginning of the pandemic, Therman had moved in and made it his headquarters.

From the outside, the house looked like any other in this sleepy Boston suburb. Inside, it could pass for a typical vacation cottage on the Atlantic coast. Underneath its back yard, however, lay an underground passage that led from the basement to the sea. Halfway to the shore, the subterranean passage widened into a cave which had stored whisky during Prohibition. Now this this twenty-foot chamber held Therman's operations center—computers, a heating unit, lights, desk, bed, and file cabinets.

The entire history of Berserker was contained there, and there were enough provisions to last for days without surfacing. The office was protected from the Atlantic entrance by video monitoring and a solid metal door. The passage from the house was secured by state-of-the-art security and response systems.

Today Therman used the office to speak with Jane Russo, a woman whose rise to power in the patriot group Oath Takers had been remarkable. "You're a lucky woman," Therman said when her face filled his Zoom screen. "I have big plans for your Oath Takers."

"Then why won't you show me your face?" she replied, staring into the camera.

Therman's first impulse was to tell Jane to screw herself and terminate the interview, but he thought again. This woman had fought her way to control of the Oath Takers in two months, ascending to a position of leadership by skill and ruthlessness that had become legendary.

He tried a conciliatory tone. "The video is off because it's better if you don't know a lot about me. Deniability. Consider me a friend trying to help you achieve your goals."

"You know my name and I don't know yours? And excuse me, but you have no real idea what my goals are."

"*To defend the Constitution against all enemies, foreign and domestic,* as I understand it. Isn't that your oath?"

"Just mouthing back something you read doesn't cut it," Jane said. "I have goals not included in that oath. One of them is not to get arrested. Can you prove you're not a government agent? The FBI is giving my group all sorts of trouble for the January sixth Capitol attack. A member of my group is in jail right now and can't get out on bail."

"I can't prove anything to you, and I'm not going to try," Therman said. "You're either in or out. In, we can talk. Out, now is the time to exit." He reached for the *leave meeting* button.

No response from Jane for a few seconds as his hand

hovered over the icon. Then, "OK, I'm in," Jane said. "What's the deal?"

"Do you know why I'm talking to you at all?" Therman said.

"Because I—"

"Wrong," Therman said. "It has nothing to do with you. The ex-president told me you were a reliable employee. Did some cleanup for him in Washington last year. That's enough for me."

"The country made a big mistake in pretending he didn't win re-election."

"What did you do for him exactly?"

"Worked as a Secret Service agent at the White House. Carried out a few special assignments I'm not going to discuss. I quit when I realized he was gone for good. Came back to this bar in Ohio. Kind of good for me, because I was here during the Capitol protest."

"My sources tell me you arranged for the Oath Takers to have a boatload of ammunition and guns ready to cross the Potomac if they were needed for the final push at the Capitol."

"I'm not saying what I did or didn't do. What's your plan?" Jane asked.

"You know how close the Capitol attack came to achieving its goal. Remember congressmen and senators hiding under seats?"

"Of course. But what do you have that would make a takeover different now?" Therman detected slight excitement in her voice. "With our former leader blocked from

social media and probably going to prison, your new ingredient would have to be damned good. What do you have that
he didn't?"

Therman rankled at the thought of being compared to
the sociopath he used to advise. "Something that will give
us a second chance. That's more than you'll have if you tell
anyone else what I'm about to say."

"Now you're the one who'll have to trust," Jane said. "My
army record speaks for itself."

"I want to organize the patriot groups in this country to
reclaim the government," Therman said.

"Don't we all. Why do you think you can actually do it?"

Therman continued. "Picture 'spontaneous' violent
uprisings on July fourth all around the country. Dozens of
state houses and the Capitol taken over, with aggression that
make January sixth look like a party. Both state and national representatives terrified for their lives. The situation will
be perfect for a strong man to take over, and I have just the
strong man in mind."

"Sounds good," Jane said. "But there's a lot more difficulty since the Capitol events of January sixth."

"Which is why we've added a totally new ingredient, a
compound that makes peaceful demonstrators go berserk."

Jane said. "I heard rumors but I'll believe it when I see it."

"We got a preview earlier this year in Paris. I can send
you the secure video link. The stuff works. Meanwhile, I
need a smart person loyal to me at my side," Therman said.
"You might be a candidate."

"Someone to get stuff done rather than sit around

talking?"

"Something like that."

"Maybe my military days could return," Jane said, looking at the ceiling. "Loved the time I spent in Afghanistan."

She seemed to catch herself. "But you'll still have to convince me."

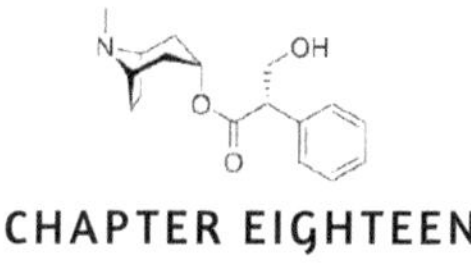

CHAPTER EIGHTEEN

PROUD MEN

MANHATTAN, NY
APRIL 19, 2021

"The cops love us—that's one big reason you should make us the lead in your July fourth storm," Joseph Riggs said to Therman as they passed the security officer in the new World Trade Center complex. His mask muffled his words slightly, but Therman had no trouble understanding him. They had been friends even before Riggs became the leader of the Proud Men.

Therman surveyed the crowd around them. Among the dozens of people lined up at six-foot intervals for the elevator to the One World Observatory, no one seemed to be paying attention to their conversation. Despite that, he cautioned Riggs not to say anything further until they arrived at the observation deck.

A smiling Asian-American woman welcomed them to the elevator entrance. "Sixty seconds to travel one hundred two stories," she said. "When you get out, you will be in a room whose window shades will gradually open. Don't be impatient. After a few seconds you will be able to see all Manhattan before you."

The elevator held only twelve people because of social distancing. Therman remembered when fifty crowded on to it before the COVID restrictions.

The only sign of the elevator's rapid ascent was the popping of Therman's ears. As they arrived at the observation floor 1250 feet above the street, Riggs said, voice low. "The main reason you want to invest in us is that we have a track record."

"Let's find a quiet corner," Therman said. The window shade in front of them slowly opened to reveal a spectacular vista of Manhattan— the East River, Brooklyn, Hudson River, midtown Manhattan as far as Central Park.

The group moved out of the arrivals area and entered the capacious observation floor. Therman guided Riggs to a side location where they would not be overheard. He had allowed a one-on-one meeting with Riggs, but he began to doubt the wisdom of that decision. There was too big a risk of being overheard and recorded.

"In the January sixth Capitol attack," Riggs continued, "we had a bunch of amateurs getting in our way. If we had been alone, we would have taken hostages, maybe gotten to the Speaker of the House and the Vice President, and killed a few Congress bastards."

"Are there any other reasons to give the Proud Men the central position?" Therman asked. "After all, you're talking about a big donation. I want to know my money is being well spent."

Riggs tilted his head. "We've shown we can produce. Look at Charleston, Portland, and Providence in the last year."

"Despite the cops?"

"Absolutely. In fact, with their approval. We're doing our job to protect America from leftists and socialists. The police are on our side. We're all patriotic Americans, strong, clean. We believe in a white America not contaminated by Hispanics, Blacks, Jews, or Asians." He flexed his biceps and smiled.

In his heart, Therman agreed with Riggs. He had allowed the Proud Men leader to have the only in-person meeting of his group recruitments because he had known him for years. He was inclined to appoint Riggs to lead the attack on America. But he had to have proof to support his inclination. "Any other reason to allow you to be the dominant players in our government takeover?" Therman asked.

"We have the experience and track record. Who's the competition? I don't think there is anyone, really."

"The Oath Takers," Therman said.

Riggs snorted. "Do you realize they are led by a woman? That by itself should disqualify them."

"Their ranks include army and police personnel. Your followers are just an assortment of male patriots," Therman said, playing devil's advocate. "I'm not sure your guys have the tactical and disciplinary capacity we need."

"You wouldn't be meeting with me if you really believed that. The Proud Men have demonstrated their commitment to disruption of the present government at every level."

"Are you ready for a throwdown?"

"A throwdown. What, specifically?"

"I'll give the groups a challenge and let them battle it out. Sort of a big fight club."

"What would the challenge be?"

"I'm working on it, but you'll know later this week. You might have to compete with the Oath Takers on at least one of the challenges."

Therman looked out over the breathtaking vista of the Hudson River that stretched below him. By the time he got to the view of the Statue of Liberty he had made up his mind. Trial by combat it would be, and he knew the target.

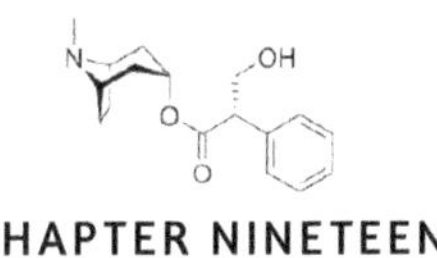

CHAPTER NINETEEN

THE THROWDOWN

MANHATTAN, NY
APRIL 22-24, 2021

Jane Russo smiled at the Zoom screen as she watched her so-called mystery boss outline the rules for deciding which patriot group would lead the takeover. She had long since discovered that Steve Therman, a dumb-ass radio host, was in fact leading the insurrection plot.

She did not know how many groups were competing, but the donor gave them three challenges. First, to plant a device looking like a bomb in the Statue of Liberty's head: second, a week later to contaminate New York's water supply with a harmless chemical that turned its color red: finally, a month after that, to create apparently spontaneous uprisings in five states at the same time. The combined goal was to increase public anxiety while he amassed enough Berserker powder to make the final push. The winner of the throwdowns would lead the nationwide July fourth disruption.

The Statue of Liberty task had to be done first. The precise directive was to plant a sealed metal tube at least ten inches long and two inches wide at the top of the staircase of the Statue of Liberty. Not an actual bomb. The goal was to instill fear and doubt, not to cause damage. Yet.

Jane knew the only significant rival in the competition was the Proud Men. The other groups were small and idealistic and had little concept of creating an effective movement. The QAnon crowd were a bunch of disorganized wackos. She had studied every patriot movement she could research. She knew what she had to do.

Therman had told her and Riggs they would have the first opportunity for the Statue of Liberty challenge. They would have to work out the details together.

Jane assumed this was a test of collaborative ability to choose the eventual leader of the plan. She also knew that a woman would come out second in any such test—hard for her to be a good ol' boy.

She and Riggs, the Proud Men leader, chose Battery Park at the south end of Manhattan to discuss the plan. They met two days after the challenge had been described. A cold wind blew across New York Bay, scattering paper wrappers and old leaves. The horns of the ferries crossing the bay mingled with the sounds of constant traffic.

"We want the first go at planting the fake bomb," Riggs said, "because our network is bigger than yours, and we can get mobilized faster. We can make the move tomorrow. Here's the device we're going to plant."

He handed over a metal tube. Jane examined it, opened the cap at its end, and surreptitiously affixed a small homing device to its wall. She sealed it again with the comment, "Looks like it fits the bill. Are you going to position it yourself?"

"No way. I'm too well known. One of our new recruits

who already works for the National Park Service will do it. Very simple, really. He'll climb the Statue of Liberty staircase carrying the tube when he does the routine clearance of the platform. At the top, he'll 'discover' the device and report with grave concern that someone seemed to have gotten this tube through security."

"Very cool. What time does the daily inspection occur?"

"Eight a.m. Like clockwork. Gets the statue ready for any VIP visitors."

"Got to hand it to you, Riggs. No way we could match that. Congratulations."

"I thought it was pretty good myself," Riggs said with a smirk. "How are you planning to get your fake bomb planted?"

"No idea. Good luck."

Jane walked over to the Staten Island ferry terminal and picked up a packet she had left in storage there. She proceeded to a nearby hotel with a rooftop lounge now closed because of COVID-19. She checked in under a false name and realized the hotel was less than half full. In the afternoon, she visited the roof. She picked the lock to the entrance door and confirmed that the path she planned to launch would be unobstructed. She returned to her room and watched TV for the rest of the evening.

The next morning at 7:55, she took the elevator to the lounge and unpacked her Hawk and Little rocket launcher. The sounds of traffic emerging from the Carey Tunnel blocked out extraneous noise as she disabled the security cameras. She set her system up and launched the missile, watching it arc across lower Manhattan and lock into its target.

At 8:01 it exploded after penetrating the thin copper skin of the Statue of Liberty and tracking to the metal tube, leaving a gaping hole.

Dressed in slacks and designer jacket and carrying the rocket launcher in a trombone case, she took a path out the back of the hotel that avoided security cameras. A dumpster three blocks from the hotel received the wiped case and its content with a spurt of dust, and she piled debris on top to cover it completely. She was on the Newark PATH line as the first news of the explosion hit the media. Her flight to Boston left within an hour of her arrival at Liberty International Airport in Newark.

She watched the investigation of the bombing unfold with the detached interest of an artist examining her work. FBI, Park Rangers, and New York Police swarmed everywhere over the Statue of Liberty. Early reports revealed ties of a dead National Park Service officer to the Proud Men, and their leader was being sought for questioning.

Part one of her plan had gone smoothly.

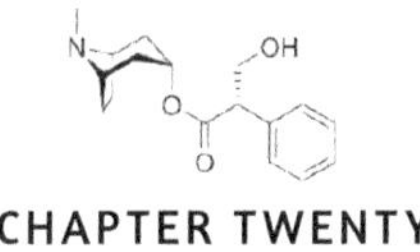

CHAPTER TWENTY

CONFRONTATION IN WINTHROP

WINTHROP, MA
APRIL 24, 2021

In his Winthrop command center, Therman heard about the Statue of Liberty explosion minutes after it happened. Riggs called to report that a ranger had been killed and the connection to the Proud Men was now public. "It had to be that bitch Jane," Riggs continued, "She was the only person who knew our plans."

Therman agreed. He had to eliminate her. He could not tolerate a subordinate who disobeyed his orders.

The problem was that he had to find her first. A tracer on her cell phone came up with nothing. He put his people on the top priority task of tracking her down.

Sitting in his cave, he watched the security camera showing the Atlantic entrance to his cave black out. "Shit," he said and cursed the camera. "An electronic failure when I need the security the most." Angry and frustrated, he shouted at the computer, "I'll find you, Jane. It's just a matter of time."

A shattering blast catapulted him from his seat, followed by a plume of smoke. The door to the seaside tunnel ripped open with a roar, raising an acrid cloud of dust and debris.

His computers rose off their desks as if some giant had smashed them. The lights went out.

The smoke stung his eyes and throat. He rose from his desk to make out what was happening behind the obscuring cloud. This could not be accidental. The density of the veil meant both an explosive charge and smoke bomb.

Blinded, he sat back in his chair and fumbled in the desk drawer for his Glock. The whirring of the emergency generators kicked in, but the debris and smoke still obscured everything.

"Freeze," a woman's voice said.

Therman's heart raced at the command. He knew that voice. He wrapped his fingers around the handle of the Glock just as he felt the cool impression of metal against the back of his head.

"Turn around. Slowly," she said. Therman swiveled and shot blindly into the cloud, but his arm was propelled upward by a powerful kick as he fired. His gun discharged into the ceiling.

A pistol slashed across his forehead. Blood dripped into his eyes. The kick propelled him from the chair and deposited him on the ground clutching his rib cage and panting. Excruciating pain accompanied every breath.

A hand from the cloud snatched his Glock away.

The smoke thinned slightly, and he twisted his head to look at the woman who had invaded his sanctuary. Jane Russo stood at the other end of a Magnum revolver. In wet suit, goggles, headlight, and gas mask, she looked like an alien predator.

"If you didn't hold the key to the Berserker powder, I'd kill you right now," she said.

"How did you get in?" Therman asked, furious but also fearful. He tried to stop the bleeding from his forehead by pressing with his bloody hands, then scrabbled around on the floor to find something to stop the bleeding.

"I'm changing your plans" Jane said.

"You should be killed for your disobedience," Therman said.

"Who's holding the gun, you piece of shit? Here's my condition for keeping you alive. Put me in charge and drop your other stupid challenges. I've looked into Berserker powder. Your plan might work, but only if I run the show."

"No way. There are more than eight hundred hate groups to be recruited. You have no power in their eyes. I'm going to use all of them, and you're irrelevant."

"The FBI has infiltrated them all. Your plan is a recipe for disaster." As she spoke, a rumble began from the tunnel leading from the sea. "Put me in charge and and I'll get you what you want." She looked behind her as the passage she had just arrived through imploded. "You have about three seconds to answer—yes or no."

Before Therman could say anything, the roof of the cave began to collapse around them. "You've destabilized the entire tunnel," he shouted as he staggered toward the passageway to the house.

Dirt and timbers hit the earth around him. Observing the exit Therman was heading for, Jane raced ahead, passed through, and slammed it behind her. By the time Therman arrived, half the room had disappeared; his computers were covered with dirt, and the security system wailed incessantly. He knew that some of his thugs might appear shortly in response to the alarm, but if he was dead that would be little use.

He pounded on the door. "I'll do whatever you say. Just let me through." A falling beam missed him by a few inches and dirt splattered on his face.

Jane's arm appeared, pushing the door open again. Therman squeezed through. He saw the entire roof collapse as the door closed behind him.

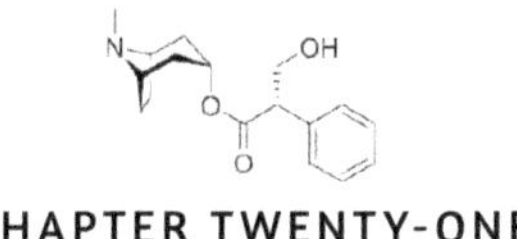

CHAPTER TWENTY-ONE

MAC AT WORK

BOSTON, MA
APRIL 26, 2021

In April, Mac returned to academic neurosurgical life. His fibular fracture healed enough to allow him to discard the splint. He worked steadily toward his usual weekly rhythm of patient care, research, teaching, and administration.

Monday at eight a.m., he and his administrative assistant Sheila previewed the weekly schedule. He would spend the rest of the day on administrative issues—recommendation letters for faculty and students, Zoom meetings, other phone calls and email. Tuesday and Thursday, he performed surgery. Nothing else could be booked on those days. Wednesday, he kept protected for laboratory research, teaching, and writing, and Friday for the brain tumor clinic. Saturdays and Sundays were blocked off for family, but he often worked to catch up at home.

"What's the nine o'clock interview today for?" he asked Sheila as they sat in his office on Monday April twenty-sixth.

"An article for the hospital's magazine to highlight the Brain Tumor Center. The hospital would like to move attention away from COVID now that the numbers seem to be diminishing."

"Isn't half an hour enough?"

"You don't have to use the whole hour. I thought you should have a little padding to your schedule this week because you're on call for emergencies," Sheila said. "And there are already some unanticipated requests for your time. Abe Mufti is waiting outside. He wanted to see you first thing and seemed upset. Julia Pedroza asked for an urgent meeting after that."

Sheila left as Dr. Mufti entered. "One of my goddammed patients is suing me," Mufti said, standing across the desk from Mac and staring down at him. "I want you testify on my behalf."

"What's the case?" Mac asked.

"A skull base meningioma we spent twenty hours removing three years ago. The tumor was wrapped around nerves and arteries. The young woman had post-operative deficits I thought would be temporary, but they haven't gotten better."

"What kind of deficits?"

"Can't swallow, requires a permanent trach. No hearing on the left, and her face is paralyzed. I need you to confirm that these are expected and sometimes necessary consequences of management for this tumor."

"Abe, you know my opinion about big surgery with a strong likelihood of bad deficits. For me, a postop intact patient is more important than a great-looking MRI with a disabled human because of surgery."

"You've got to testify for me anyway. My lawyers say you're the most credible witness in the country to support me."

"But I can't support you. I don't agree with what you did."

"If I didn't remove the whole tumor, it would come back."

"Didn't it come back anyway?"

"Yes, but it would have recurred sooner if I didn't take it out. And it turned out to be an aggressive meningioma."

"It sounds like the patient didn't think it was worth the deficit."

"Patients don't know anything. As surgeons, we have to make the difficult decisions. And I'm the only person in this department who can perform the kind of big surgery we're talking about here, so don't talk to me about complications."

Mac stood. "Abe, I'm sorry, but I would be a bad expert witness. Your surgery takes too long, exhausts nurses and operating room technicians, and hurts patients. Your ideas are twenty years old. There are better ways of treating these tumors today."

"Radiation? Focused ultrasound? Micro-embolization? Deliberately leave tumor behind? Useless. Big surgery is the only answer."

"We'll have to disagree." Mac said.

"I told my lawyers you'd say this," Mufti said. "You don't have the guts to do what I do anyway."

"This meeting is over," Mac said.

Mufti stomped out, slamming the door behind him.

Sheila reappeared. "Is everything OK? I've never seen Abe look that angry."

"We had a philosophical disagreement," Mac said. "When is Dr. Pedroza coming?"

Mac was always glad to see Julia. Her concern for her

patients combined with a commitment to research and teaching mirrored Mac's philosophy.

"She just called to check how your day was going. Should be here in five minutes."

"Did she seem OK?"

"Anxious. Not angry. Not like Abe."

As he waited, Mac's gaze slid to the diplomas and certificates hanging on his wall. Best Doctors, Surgeon Select, Patient Preferred, Boston's Best, all acknowledged his standing with patients. Certificates of honor from dozens of groups and forums in neurosurgery around the world testified to his international respect, as did his Membership in the Academy of Medicine, Fellowship in the College of Surgeons of Scotland, and Associateship of Royal Society of Medicine of the UK. A bookshelf packed with professional books, a dozen edited by him, sat beside a file cabinet with raw data and final drafts of three hundred professional articles he had authored or co-authored. Piles of paper strewn on his desk threatened to engulf photographs of his family and a computer monitor. With its orderly disorganization, the office reflected his own complex life.

He could have a much nicer office if he were in private practice, but he didn't care. The challenge of advancing knowledge, teaching others, and using new technology to help patients with complex tumors other surgeons could not deal with made him enthusiastic about each day.

He almost didn't hear Sheila announce Julia Pedroza, who entered with hesitation. She twisted her hands as she stood in front of the desk.

"Let's get a breath of fresh air," Mac said, realizing that this was not a routine meeting.

They left the hospital through a back exit leading directly to the water. Cool sea air carried the scents of salt and fish. Seagulls swooped and squawked, and boats zigzagged across the water.

"We've started the search for chief," Julia said as they strolled along the Harborwalk, "and Max Eli is trying to sabotage your candidacy from the get-go. He keeps harping on the amount of time you spend away from the hospital."

"I couldn't give up my work in emerging countries," Mac said. "For me, it's more important than being chief."

Julia stopped and stared at him. "Mac, it would be a disaster for someone outside our group to become chief. That's why I wanted to meet with you. I'm already having serious reservations about my career. When Carlos and I moved from Bogota, I wanted to do academic neurosurgery because of you. Teaching, research, and patient care seemed a great calling, and I was willing to repeat my training here to learn how to do it."

"But now?" Mac asked gently.

"I see how much dysfunction there is in the system. And I see how hard you work. And how little time you have for your family."

"And you think it's too difficult? I wouldn't trade this life for anything."

She looked at him with tears forming in her eyes. "I just found out I'm pregnant."

She paused to let the news sink in. Mac invited her to sit on one of the benches along the walk and took a seat beside her. "How wonderful," he said. "Carlos must be ecstatic."

"He is, but he's also worried about me burning out. Surgeon, wife, and mother are already three jobs. Adding research and teaching is too much."

"I'm not going to try to persuade you about anything," Mac said. "All I can tell you is that for me there is no other calling than academic neurosurgery." He turned to point to the beautiful brick and glass hospital gleaming in the morning sun. "Look at our professional home, Julia, a monument to the hope that we can diminish human suffering. We must maintain that ideal, keep learning about the diseases we face, and transmit our knowledge to others. Research and teaching are necessary if you care about patients."

"But can one person do clinical practice, research, and teaching?"

"If anyone can, you can. It takes discipline, and an ability to say *no*. Your work on brain imaging has already made a difference, and you're uniquely qualified to advance that field. Just think how important your imaging of the hypothalamus was when we had the hypothalamic hamartoma patient last year."

They started back toward the hospital. "Everyone in academics will help you wherever we can. I hope you'll stay with your original dream."

"Thanks, Mac. I'll talk with Carlos about what you said. One thing for sure. If it weren't for you, I wouldn't even keep trying."

Mac had no idea whether he had convinced Julia to stay in the academic world. He returned to his office concerned. Only through ongoing generations of surgeons could the proud tradition of neurosurgery be continued.

"This is Mary Blandon of the Harbor Gazette," Sheila said as Mac came through the office door.

He looked at the young woman with iPhone at the ready. "You're early," he said.

"I couldn't wait," she said. "May I come in?"

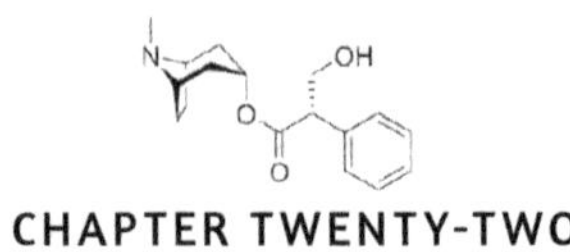

CHAPTER TWENTY-TWO

GUNSHOTS

HARBOR HOSPITAL
APRIL 26, 2021

"OK if I record our interview?" the young journalist asked as she sat in the chair Julia had just vacated.

"Of course."

"Sheila said we might be cut short because you're on emergency call, so I'll begin with the hard question first. This article is going to be about brain tumors. Is having a brain tumor a death sentence?"

"No. Half the tumors we deal with can be removed completely and safely."

"I've done some research. Those are the meningiomas, vestibular schwannomas, and pituitary adenomas?"

"Yes, and some rare tumors like hypothalamic hamartomas."

"What about gliomas? Can they be cured?"

"If they are caught as low-grade gliomas in a young person and removed, they can at least be put into long term remission. If they are a particular type called oligodendroglioma they can be treated with surgery and chemotherapy with a very good outlook."

"So even gliomas aren't always fatal?"

"Correct, though the glioblastoma, the most malignant tumor of the brain, has no good treatment."

"What about brain tumors in children?"

"The most histologically malignant of these, the medulloblastoma, can be put into long term remission with surgery, radiation, and chemotherapy. Craniopharyngiomas, rare tumors, can be cured by surgery. And some gliomas have a good outlook in children."

The hospital public address crackled into activity. *Doctor Duncan MacGregor to the emergency room stat, Doctor Duncan MacGregor to the emergency room.*

"Sorry," Mac said. "I'm on call, so I have to go. Perhaps Sheila can set up another appointment."

When Mac arrived in the emergency room a few minutes later, the nurse-in-charge shook her head and pointed to trauma room one. "It's a mess," she said.

Doctors and nurses swarmed around a stretcher. Shouted orders, the clanging of monitors, blood on the floor and on sheets, and the odor of disinfectant created a mélange Mac never quite go used to.

"What happened?" Mac asked the resuscitation team leader.

"Young Black guy wandered into the wrong neighborhood in New Hampshire. Three homeowners with guns called for him to stop. He ran. They shot him."

Mac moved to the patient, noting the gunshot wounds to chest and head. The thoracic surgeon had opened an incision between ribs and was massaging the victim's heart directly.

"Hemothorax," the surgeon said. "No use wasting time with epinephrine and external chest massage. We drained the blood and are getting some cardiac output with direct cardiac massage, but we need you to look at his head to see if anything is recoverable."

Mac moved to the top of the stretcher. The front of the victim's head had been blown off by the exit bullet— forehead and eyes gone, brain and blood spilling onto the pillow.

Mac gowned and gloved and lifted the head to show the back of the skull. "Here's the entry point," he said. "A bullet from behind."

"Same with the chest. Shot in the back. Assault rifle." the thoracic surgeon said.

"How did he end up in Massachusetts?" Mac asked.

"COVID patients occupied all the beds in New Hampshire hospitals. They needed a sophisticated team to sort out what to do, so we offered to take him."

"The head wound killed him instantaneously," Mac said. "There's nothing to resuscitate. No need for a brain death protocol here."

"That's all we needed to hear, Mac. Thanks," the thoracic surgeon said. "I just don't understand what the crazies who shoot someone like this are thinking."

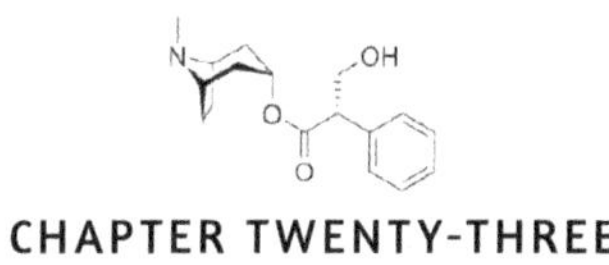

CHAPTER TWENTY-THREE

WOLF MILITIA

POTTERVILLE, MICHIGAN
MAY 5-6, 2021

On May 5, 2021, Jimmy Blair led his girlfriend Carla O'Malley to a basement room of the shuttered high school in Potterville, Michigan. He was dressed in jeans, black hoodie, and work boots, and carried a Remington Model 700 American Hunter rifle. She wore the same outfit minus the firearm.

"This is where we'll do it," Blair said. "This is where we'll execute our governor." Matter of fact. No emotion.

"I studied video journalism in this room," O'Malley said. She looked around at the soundproofing tiles that covered the walls and ceiling. "Potterville High's own broadcasting studio. The broadcast desk was right where that chair is. The video camera's there in the corner. Three years ago. Seems a century."

She turned back. "The school's been closed for a year. How'd you get a key?"

"Pocketed it while I was here," Blair said with pride in his voice. "Kept it for four years. Never realized it would help me now."

He moved to the wall and gestured. "Here's how it'll go

down. We'll kidnap the governor from her home in Lansing, put a black bag over her head, and tie her up with zip ties. Should only take ten minutes to get here."

He pointed to the chair in the center of the room. "We'll put her in that chair, interrogate her with the camera running, then execute her. You'll record the video but we'll only send it to YouTube after we get rid of the body. We'll leave it broadcasting on a loop from here. No one will be able to trace it to us."

O'Malley looked worried. "What if they track us down, Jimmy? Look what they did to the Wolverines. Followed their trail all the way to Munith."

"We're smarter than the Wolverines. Bear Militia hasn't been in the news yet and no one realizes we have access to the school."

"But how do you know we'll be safe?"

"All's I know is that our bitch governor will get what she deserves for her lockdowns and mask mandates and school closings." Blair pointed his rifle at the chair and fired.

The sound blasted his eardrums and reverberated in the room despite the soundproofing. He could almost see the figure of the dead governor slump in the chair. That image filled him with delight.

People always called him a loser. Executing the governor would change all that. He would be Somebody.

The bullet lodged in the opposite wall too deep to retrieve. He looked over at O'Malley, who had covered her ears and now glared at him with wild eyes.

"Are you crazy, Jimmy?" she asked, turning to the door

as if expecting someone to appear. "No way we can carry this off. The cops will be all over us."

Blair impaled her with a dagger stare. "That's what everyone thought about the Capitol attack. Look what happened. Piece of cake to get in. The opposition is soft."

He moved closer, got in her face. "Wait a minute. You chickening out?"

O'Malley stepped back, took a deep breath. "We both hate our governor, but here's no way we'll be able to do this. How will you get into her house, for instance?"

Blair gave her a knowing smile. "We'll have magic powder."

"Magic powder?"

"Stuff called Berserker powder. Makes people who drink it go crazy. One of my buds in the Oath Takers told me. We're going to use it in Lansing on the day of The Storm."

"Use it where? How? What does it do?"

Blair had to decide whether to trust O'Malley. He thought of the plans they had hatched together, their rifle shoots, their communications with other patriot groups on Parler. "Look, you've got to promise to keep what I'm going to tell you now a secret."

"Have I ever done different?" She looked pissed.

"You think the fighting at the Capitol was good?"

"Of course, but it took months for the president to stoke it. He's not going to be around to do that here."

"Exactly. This magic powder gets the same result. Come with me and I'll show you."

They exited the building and piled into a dilapidated

utility truck marked *Potterville General Store.* April rains had turned the dirt road into mud. They turned into the empty parking lot of the general store.

"Jimmy, when're you gonna get a real place," O'Malley asked, stumbling as she descended from the truck. "Not live under the store like a rat?"

Blair gave the usual answer as they crunched toward his door. "Easy for you to say. You got a cushy waitress job and live with your family. My family kicked me out. The Democrats have given all the jobs to immigrants, so I only have unemployment to live on. Hardly keeps me in booze and ammo, let alone food for the dogs." He turned to her with a sly smile. "That'll change, though. The guy I'm talking about will give us money along with his magic powder."

They stepped down the wooden steps into the room. The stench of urine whacked him as it always did. He shook his head, angry again that immigrants made him live in an unfinished basement with exposed plumbing, little heat, and bare incandescent bulbs. A sink with dirty dishes, toilet, and plastic shower stall finished the décor. And this shithole also had to be headquarters for the Wolf Militia while he was getting ready to put them on the map.

"How much money?" O'Malley asked.

"Guess." Blair checked on his dogs. The largest one, part Labrador, lay on the bed, really a mattress on the floor surrounded by dirty sheets. The other two, mutts harder to identify, huddled in the dark corners. Keeping those mouths fed was a constant problem for him but stealing food from the store above helped.

"Ten thousand dollars?" O'Malley moved into the militia area of the basement, marked off with two folding chairs. A floor plan of the Michigan State Capitol with a red circle around the central portion hung on the wall. Several rifles and shotguns leaned against the map. A table sat littered with a variety of booklets and scraps of paper.

She picked up a rifle.

"Fifty times that," Blair replied with a smirk.

"Five hundred thousand?" O'Malley said, almost dropping the rifle. "That's too much, Jimmy. Anybody who's going to pay that is looking for big results, maybe a lot of deaths."

"Of course. What do you expect when the boogaloo comes?" Blair asked.

"You mean these people really mean to start a civil war?"

"What else?" Blair stared at O'Malley again. Had she been jerking him around all this time about hating the system and wanting to overthrow it?

He moved swiftly toward her, but she had the gun raised and ready. "Don't come any closer, Jimmy. I know how you get when you're angry like this. You blow up and hurt things and then feel terrible a couple of days later. I'm walking out the door now. I'm not saying I won't help with what you have in mind, but I want to think about it."

"If I hear you've told anyone about our plans, I will personally kill you, and maybe your family too." Jimmy could feel the surge of anger build. He had always assumed his bitch would follow him to the death.

At the door, O'Malley stopped. "I suggest you get in

touch with this guy and find out what the real situation is. Until then, don't come near me or my family."

Blair didn't bother to follow her after the door closed. The town was so small he could easily drop by her house with a five-minute walk. Instead, he tracked down the contact information for the Winthrop man with the money.

He called the number and left a message on the machine. "This here's Jimmy Blair from the Wolf Militia. I want to talk with you about your magic powder." He waited the rest of the day in his basement, pacing and talking to his dogs about what he was going to do when he got the $500,000.

The return call came three hours later. He didn't like it. First off, the person's voice was electronically altered. Second, whoever it was had an attitude. They didn't seem to understand what the Wolf Militia was capable of, given the right funding. Blair felt his temper flaring. "Listen, you bag of shit," he shouted into the phone. "I can trace this number and find you. The Wolf Militia is going to get a piece of this action. If you don't think so, I'm just going to add you to our kill list. And maybe I'll just tell the authorities about your plan."

He hung up, satisfied and proud. Those guys would know he was Someone now.

He heard a knock on the door about two the next afternoon. He opened to a woman with short-cropped black hair wearing army fatigues with Oath Takers insignia.

"I'm Jane," she said. "Are you with the Wolf Militia?"

"With them? Hell, I'm their leader," he said.

"May I come in? I wanted to discuss a distribution of funds."

"Of course." Now he would get the money and recognition he deserved. Five hundred thousand dollars—that would make his family sit up and take notice. He turned away to lead his guest to one of the wooden chairs. When he turned back, he stared at the barrel of a Glock 17 pistol, complete with suppressor.

"We've decided not to fund your application."

Blair saw the muzzle flash, heard a puff, then saw and felt nothing.

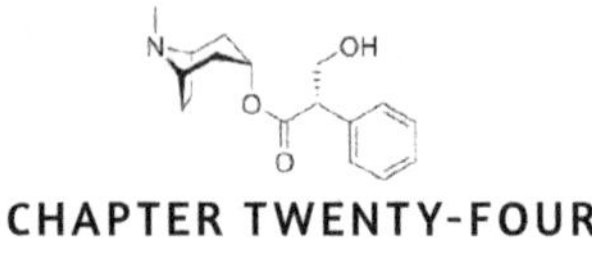

CHAPTER TWENTY-FOUR

TANGER MED

MOROCCO
MAY 14, 2021

Therman congratulated himself as he stood on the bridge of his ship *Sakinah*, now occupying mooring S43 in the vast container facility called Tanger Med. The King of Morocco had created this Atlantic port to reinforce Morocco's place as a world commercial and shipping power.

It had worked well into Therman's plans. Located just outside the Straits of Gibraltar, it provided perfect access to the Americas, Europe, and Africa. Therman's small container ship was hardly a blip on the nine million tons passing through the port each year. Now a floating pharmaceutical manufacturing plant, it would soon be a distribution facility too.

Since the confrontation in Winthrop, he and Jane had developed a wary collaboration. Jane had convinced him that a small group of dedicated operatives would be safer than dozens of disparate patriot groups. The Oath Takers, with branches all over the United States, would become the activators of The Storm on July fourth. They would provide the mechanism to create chaos, and he knew from his own experience that she would keep them on task.

She turned out to be an intelligent collaborator. He could continue manufacturing and stockpiling the drug while she carried out day-to-day management.

He abandoned the Winthrop house, with its tunnels collapsed and filled with debris. That would arouse less suspicion than trying to repair it or retrieve files. He did not need to be associated with it any further, since he had a floating command center in the *Sakinah.*

"I have to admit Tanger Med is a spectacular setting, but it was a pain in the ass to get here from Potterville," Jane said as she joined Therman on the bridge. "And will we have enough product to distribute before July fourth?"

"I told you we'll be ready, and we will. We have the sailors and workers we need. We've also added more officers from the Tangier police force to our payroll to make sure we have no leaks. You just better have the Oath Takers primed and loaded."

"Don't worry, they'll be ready. What about the Moroccan policewoman who discovered our land facility?"

"She's been on personal leave for two weeks since Paris, and when she returns, she will be assigned to the outskirts of Tangier. She won't have the resources to investigate anything."

"When do we sail?" Jane asked.

"Tomorrow night at eleven p.m. Arrive in Boston in ten days and begin our distribution to the rest of the country right away. That gives us plenty of time to be ready."

"And you still think Boston's container facility can handle this?"

"Absolutely. The Conley terminal is small but adequate. And no one would expect it to be the center of a national distribution of a drug that will destroy the country. You remember the 9/11 attacks? The people involved started in airports where no one imagined a problem. That's what we're counting on. This ship is just a medium size container vessel making a scheduled landing. Nothing to mark it special. No, our plan is foolproof. And on July fourth, America will self-destruct. With our help."

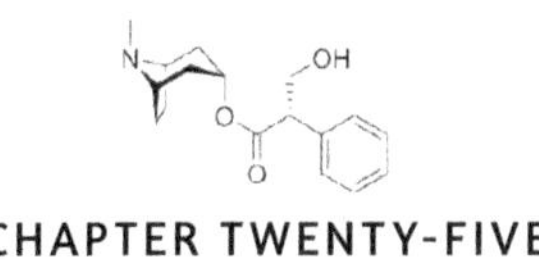

CHAPTER TWENTY-FIVE

KIDNAPPED

MOROCCO
MAY 15, 2021

After the episode at the Louvre, Amara returned to Tangier, but her frustration level increased steadily. She had seen the effects of a compound that changed humans into wild animals but she could not find out anything else. Where was it being manufactured? Who was behind its production?

Fear jolted her awake at night. She dreamed of her Moroccan neighbors and friends turning into satanic beasts and attacking her family compound. Her frustration increased when her new supervisor reassigned her to a position monitoring the villages west of Tangier along the Atlantic Coast.

"I would prefer to stay in Tangier," she said to him.

"I have made the decision," he said, turning away from her to indicate the discussion was over.

"But—" she began.

"Officer Zadi, I am your chief," her boss said. "You will do what I say or find yourself without a job."

She wondered whether, like Duroc, this chief and some of his staff had been put on the payroll of the cartel making the powder.

The only positive element of her new position was free time. She spent that time trying to track down new factories. The group responsible for the explosion in Tangier must be relocating right now to keep their production up. She journeyed to possible sites for such a building, as far away as the Atlas Mountains, the Oasis of Meknes, the bazaars of Fez, the urban sprawl of Casablanca, the elegance of Marrakech, and the business world of Rabat. She talked with friends in the police departments and called friends in Libya and Algeria. Nowhere did she discover a new drug manufacturing facility.

She found solace in watching ships coming and going from Tanger Med in their steady multinational stream. This port had changed Tangier from a sleepy end-of-the-line town to a thriving commercial center. With binoculars, she spent hours of spare time gazing at the port to survey the cadre of ships that berthed at this thriving Atlantic center.

Today she had a surprise. On the dock, she saw one of her colleagues, a lieutenant who left the Department after Duroc's death, walking along the dock. She followed him through the maze with her binoculars. He stopped at a ship called *Sakinah,* Arabic for Serenity.

Amara ran toward the man, calling his name. He looked back at her, then raced onto the boat. She pulled out her phone to call for backup, felt the blow to the back of her head, and felt her world fade to black.

Amara opened her eyes, saw only darkness, felt rough fabric encircling her head, winced at the tape over her mouth, smelled only her own perfume. She shook her head and tried to move her hands against restraints. She realized quickly that her rms and legs were bound in a chair.

Despite the heat outside, a chill engulfed her. Where was she? What had happened?

The sensation of rocking. Waves against a hull. The smell of oil.

The Sakinah.

Footsteps above pacing back and forth. A man's voice. Foreign accent. On a phone.

"Everything as planned, my brother… will not be investigating… for a while. We have her on the ship and…tomorrow. Should be distributing product…days."

She tried to move her arms and legs again, to scream through the wide tape that silenced her, to pound her feet. She shook her head back and forth. The activity seemed to make her even more confused. She fell back into unconsciousness as the questions pounded at her brain. Who had done this to her? And why? And what next?

Shouts jolted Amara awake again. She had no idea how long she had been unconscious.

"Wake up." She heard footsteps move toward her, felt a hand slap the burlap bag around her head. She lifted her eyes toward the place she thought a face would be, imagined what her assailant looked like.

She did not have to imagine long. The bag was ripped from her head.

"It's time for us to talk," a man unfamiliar to her said. "I will remove the tape from your mouth, but if you try to call out I will replace it even more firmly and whip your face with my pistol. Is that understood?"

She nodded. He was American, fat, with a Brooklyn accent and hair that seemed never to have been combed.

He ripped the tape off her lips, tearing the surface. She licked the bleeding places as he continued.

"Why were you snooping around this boat at Tanger Med?" he asked. "Who are you working for?"

"I saw one of my former colleagues and followed him to catch up," she said with some desperation in her voice. "I'm not snooping, just interested."

"You worked with Dr. Duncan MacGregor to investigate the death of a man killed by a monkey?"

"Yes."

"What did you find?"

"Nothing."

He paused and looked at her with narrowed eyelids. "Miss Amara, I am a compassionate man. I have colleagues who are not so kind. They have methods of finding out things that are—well, cruel."

"I'm telling the truth."

He sighed. "Well, we shall see."

He replaced the sack over her head. She felt the cool sensation of alcohol on her arm, the jab of a needle, then nothing.

Therman tried to ignore his colleague Hameni as they approached the door to Amara's cabin the next morning. The stubborn Moroccan woman had resisted all their attempts to find out anything. Therman wanted to increase psychological pain to the maximum by injecting the Berserker drug but keeping her restrained. Hameni wanted to try a tranquilizing drug instead.

Their argument climaxed just outside Amara's stateroom. "I say give her Berserker and watch what happens," Therman said. "She would be a perfect guinea pig. We can find out what she is experiencing and observe just how violent she will get."

"My brother," Hameni said, "That plan will not get us what we need. As you have said, we want to find out how much she knows, how many other people have this knowledge, and how deeply MacGregor is involved. Pain, at least psychological pain, doesn't seem to work. It only makes her more resistant. Do you remember Aesop's fable of The North Wind and the Sun?"

"A Greek fairy tale? Not part of my heritage," Therman snorted.

"It's universal, my brother. The question was who was stronger. The test was to tear a man's coat away from him. The wind blew and blew to blow the coat off him; the man just wrapped it around himself more firmly. In the hot sun, he removed it and gave it away. Pleasure works better than pain, and we have drugs that will create both."

"Do you have a pleasure drug with you?"

"In my pocket. Please let me show you what a little pharmacological love can do."

They entered the room to find a thin woman tied to an armchair, head on chest, eyes closed, legs spread carelessly.

Dark hair snarled into a rat's nest, face smeared with dirt. Her dress stank with urine and sweat as she moaned words they could not understand. She did not look up as they entered.

Hameni flipped some switches and moved to Amara's side, where he inserted a needle into the intravenous line.

Amara imagined she was listening to limpid strains of Chopin. The fragrance of roses caressed her nostrils. A gentle light penetrated her closed eyelids. She could feel a slight breeze as the room temperature climbed to tropical levels.

Her face relaxed into a smile. She forgot the psychic agony of last week's drug experiences. In fact, she couldn't remember anything unpleasant at all.

Her neck had no tension. Her arms floated at her side, almost disconnected from her body. Her brain was surrounded by sunlight and warmth. She could feel the gentle touch of a lover's body against hers as they lay intertwined in a nocturnal cocoon. She imagined his soft voice in her ear whispering how much he loved her, the scent of his cologne, his dark eyes. She was loved, and accomplished, and safe.

In front of her stood a dark-complexioned man, bearded, about five feet six inches tall, body covered by Saudi robes. She had no idea who he was, but he was clearly about to save her.

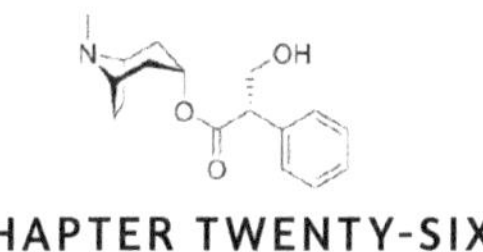

CHAPTER TWENTY-SIX

TRACKING AMARA

Even though it was six in the morning, James Brogan answered Mac's call on the first ring. "I just got a desperate message from Amara Zadi's father," Mac began. "He hasn't heard from his daughter for three days. She's never gone that long without talking to him."

"What does he think happened?" Brogan asked.

"Doesn't know, but he's convinced something's wrong."

"I assume he checked with her friends, visited her apartment?"

"Yes, all of that. He reported her absence to the Tangier police, but they haven't helped. He can't get co-operation from anyone."

"What's your impression, Mac?"

"Amara would never do anything to upset her father. I think she's been kidnapped or killed."

"Related to our investigation of the monkeys?"

"Perhaps."

"OK, let's assume the worst," Brogan said. "How can I help?"

"Track down where she was last seen."

Brogan found interrogating the chief of the Tangier police more difficult than he expected. "James Brogan of the CIA here," he began, after cutting though several layers of subordinates.

"How do I know you are who you say you are?"

"Call me back at this number. You will find it is the official CIA line."

"I do not have time for such foolishness."

"Perhaps a call from the king's office would convince you. Shall I ask for their help?"

"What's your problem?" the man asked.

"I need to get in touch with Amara Zadi."

"She has not come to work for three days. I am about to fire her."

"We're worried she might have been kidnapped."

"What concern is that of yours? Why do you Americans always think you can stick your nose in where it doesn't belong?"

"Can you tell me where and when she was last seen?"

"No."

"What do you mean, no?"

"I have no idea. She had a day off and never reported to duty after that. I expect she decided to go off somewhere more pleasant than Tangier. She has been unhappy with a new position I gave her. She used to be a good officer. Now she just complains all the time."

Brogan decided a different approach would be necessary to get any cooperation. "Monsieur, we think Amara is being targeted by an international terrorist cartel. It is of vital importance to the United States and Interpol to find out where she is. I will give you two hours to track her down. If you have done nothing in that time, I will have our ambassador take the issue up with the king. Your choice."

The line went dead. It was eight a.m. in Chelsea, Massachusetts, two p.m. in Tangier.

The Tangier police chief called him back exactly two hours later. "We tracked Officer Zadi to our port, Tanger Med, on her day off three days ago," the police chief said. "She boarded a container ship there."

"Do you have the name of the ship?" Brogan asked.

"*Sakinah*. It left Morocco later that same day."

"Its destination?"

"We do not require departing ships to provide their itineraries. That's all I have."

Brogan believed him, thanked him, and began to delve into the history of the *Sakinah*.

By the time he had finished, he realized Amara's disappearance was potentially relevant to the Berserker plot and might provide the breakthrough he had hoped for.

Through several dummy corporations, the *Sakinah* was owned by the media billionaire Rufus Morlock. Steven Therman, an American, was listed as its contact person. Therman had requested a nine-month berth in Tanger Med beginning last January, just after the factory explosion.

The ship left suddenly the day Amara had gone missing. *Why had Sakinah left Morocco so precipitously? Was Amara's disappearance connected with its early departure?*

Brogan wanted to trace the ship and intercept it. His CIA

superior nixed that idea. "Not going to happen. We don't like the optics of boarding an international ship for any reason. We're not pirates."

"Even if the ship could be harboring a drug that produces violence incredibly dangerous to the US?" Brogan asked.

"Doesn't matter. Don't even think about intercepting it."

"And the woman, Amara Zadi? Her life counts for nothing?"

"Do I have to repeat myself, Brogan? She's not a U.S. citizen. Let it go!"

Brogan had one other possibility. Steve Therman, an American citizen, gave his American address as 102 Ocean Drive in Winthrop, Massachusetts. That was just a few miles away from Brogan. Perhaps a search of that property would provide relevant information. The question was how to arrange it, and what to expect.

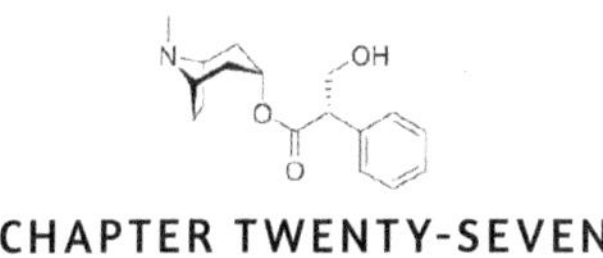

CHAPTER TWENTY-SEVEN

REVELATION

CHELSEA, MA
MAY 17-18, 2021

Brogan described his findings to the agent in charge of the regional FBI office, the man who had allowed him to have space during the investigation of the Berserker powder.

"You want us to send a SWAT team onto a man's property based on that flimsy evidence?" the agent asked. "No way. Get some real intel and bring it back to me, then I'll pass it along to regional and see what they have to say. I'm sure you're aware we've got to be careful about the public perception of our agency right now. We're not going to pay a visit to that Winthrop house any time soon."

Brogan concluded the FBI would be no help. He still wanted to look at Therman's property. He called the Winthrop police and arranged to meet with the chief at eight the next morning, arriving early at the tidy red brick headquarters on Metcalf Square.

"You Brogan?" a burly man standing in front of the building asked.

"Yep. You Chief Callahan?"

"The same," the man said, "But I was expecting someone who looked a little more Irish."

"You suggesting a Black man shouldn't have an Irish name?" Brogan asked, pretending to be offended. "My dad was Irish, came from Boherbue in County Cork. Mom was Black, from Roxbury."

"I guess you're actually more Irish than I am," Callahan said with a chuckle. "I'm third generation American. C'mon in and tell me what's going on."

Once they were in the chief's office, a cramped space piled high with papers and pictures, Brogan made his case. "As I mentioned on the phone, I work with the counter-terrorism unit of the CIA." He pulled out his creds and placed them on the table. "I'm in Boston to follow a person of interest who may be involved with an international terrorist organization. He also seems to be associated with a house on your seashore."

"His name?"

"Therman. The house is 102 Ocean Drive."

"Interesting you should mention that place. I grew up in Winthrop, but we never knew it as the Therman house. It belonged to a woman with a different name who died last year. It's odd because neighbors reported a disturbance on the property a couple of weeks ago. When we sent a squad car to investigate, the guy who answered the door said he had been tuning up his motorcycle in the basement and had a backfire. We didn't believe him but didn't have enough data to do anything."

"And since then?"

"Nothing. In fact, we haven't seen hide nor hair of anyone around the property. Based on what you've told me, I'm going to get you a warrant so we can take a look, though. We don't want terrorists hiding in our community. You're welcome to join us for the party."

At ten a.m., Brogan and two of Callahan's officers approached Therman's property from the road. Hans was a veteran of the force, Michael a junior recruit. When they arrived at the property, they found a locked gate blocking the only opening in a high stone wall surrounding the yard on three sides. The fourth side faced the ocean.

They pressed the buzzer in the gate but got no answer after several attempts. "Should we break the door down?" Michael asked.

"I have an idea," Hans said. "We can approach the property from the sea." He made a call, then drove them to a landing dock a mile away. A sturdy boat marked *Winthrop Harbor Patrol* sat moored on the quay. Hans waved at the captain, who beckoned them onto the police vessel.

Five minutes later, they arrived at the shorefront of Therman's property. "Stay in the boat," Hans said. "We'll do the recon." Brogan began to protest, but Hans and Michael jumped onto the rocky sea entrance to Therman's estate and disappeared before he could finish his sentence.

Michael signaled from the shore a few minutes later. The captain maneuvered the boat to let the two policemen clamber aboard.

"Something weird has happened on that property," Hans said. "Looks as if there was some sort of room or tunnel underground that partially collapsed. Could be dangerous."

"Any sign of occupants?' Brogan asked, hopeful that they might find someone to answer questions.

"Nope. Looks like it's been deserted for at least a couple of weeks," Hans replied. "Our chief will sure want to know what was going on under that yard, though. I'm going to talk with him as soon as we get back. I think our ultrasound guru would be appropriate."

Two hours later, Brogan rejoined the two cops at the Therman house. They opened the gate to admit a man introduced as the underground detection wizard. He surveyed the caved-in back yard with what appeared to be a mobile radar unit.

"Look," the radar man said, pointing to the images on his screen. "Some sort of office buried under the debris. Desks, computers, file cabinets, even a bed. There must have been a subterranean room under the back yard of the house."

"Can we excavate it?" Brogan asked with a note of excitement in his voice. This might provide the clues he needed to understand Therman's plot.

"I'm not sure our warrant includes digging up a collapsed back yard," Hans said. "I'll ask the chief. You should go back to your office and check in with us tomorrow morning."

When Brogan returned the next morning, a crew was digging out the collapsed room under the supervision of the chief. "We haven't had this kind of excitement for a while," Callahan said. "The woman who owned the house was Therman's sister who died last year. Couldn't reach the present owner. The judge told us we could dig out whatever's under here, taking into account your concerns and a potential danger to adjacent properties."

By noon the excavation crew had pulled out desk, computer and file cabinets identified on the ultrasound the day before.

"I need to see the hard drive from the computer," Brogan said.

"You can't," the police chief said. "Not yet. It's going to take a few days for our IT people to check it out."

"Every minute may be critical in this investigation."

Chief Callahan stared at Brogan for a minute, then said, "How about a compromise. You can look at what we've dug up, but only at the station until we've gone through the red tape to get it released."

Brogan knew that he could theoretically overrule Callahan's jurisdiction but was grateful to have experts who could help him get into the files needed.

At seven o'clock that evening, the chief stopped by the room where the material was being processed under Brogan's watchful eye. "I'm out of here," he said. "Looks like you're going to be here for a while. Our man covering the night shift will get you anything you need."

Brogan spent two more hours poring over files and information as it became available to him. As he put the pieces together, he realized he absolutely had to act that night. Amara was certainly on the *Sakinah*, along with a cargo of Berserker drug that could be unloaded anywhere. Any report Brogan filed officially would be debated and delayed in innumerable bureaucratic channels. He had to board the *Sakinah* now to find Amara and confirm it had the Berserker powder on board.

And he needed someone medically sophisticated and trustworthy to help assess Amara's medical condition. He called Mac. "I've been looking at Therman's files. He's going to use Berserker powder to cause nationwide chaos. I have to board the distribution ship tonight to confirm my hunch."

"Why are you telling me this?" Mac asked. "You need to inform your CIA guys, or the police, or someone who can stop Therman and his cronies."

"I'll inform them in due time" Brogan said. "I need more data to convince them. And there's the medical consideration. Amara is on that ship. I really need someone medical to stand by."

"Shouldn't the police do the searching?"

"The kidnappers will kill Amara and dump her body if they think there's police involvement. Could you join me at the Conley terminal at ten?"

"Hell no," Mac said. "My wife would kill me. How good is your information that Amara might be on board?'

"Impeccable." Brogan thought that small lie would be OK to get Mac to join him. "And I can guarantee she will have been tortured."

"I'll need to talk with Lauren before I can commit."

"Of course. Just be sure she knows this is potentially the biggest threat America has had for decades."

Mac called back half an hour later. "Lauren says I should do what I think is necessary. I need to rescue Amara Zadi."

"Great," Brogan replied. "Meet me at the Falcon terminal at ten."

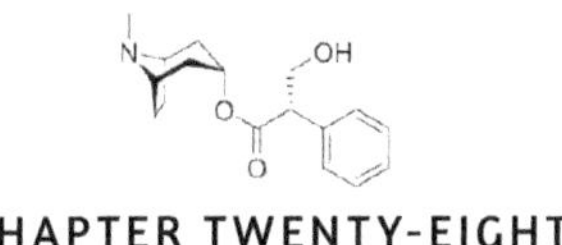

CHAPTER TWENTY-EIGHT

CONLEY CONTAINER TERMINAL

BOSTON, MA
MAY 18, 2021

Brogan and Mac met precisely at ten at the Falcon passenger terminal of the Boston Seaport. Brogan wore a leather jacket that partly concealed his wet suit. Mac wore jeans and sneakers with a black wool hat and jacket. The May night was cool with a waxing crescent of moon.

Brogan led Mac past the large passenger facility to a dark area of the dock. "Mac, we have to keep this between us," he said as he made his final preparations to slip into the Reserve Channel. "I can't officially board a ship in an American port."

His gut knotted as he realized what he was about to do. He had no time to go through regular channels, and he did not trust some of the people in the firm around him. Too many of them were from the previous administration, perhaps even favoring the attackers.

He had uncovered a domestic terrorism conspiracy more dangerous than any foreign threat to the United States. The timetable for distribution of the Berserker powder made it critical to stop the plan now. Identifying Amara's abductors might be the only way to prevent a fatal attack on the United States.

"A night visit to a foreign container ship will be hard to explain to your agency if you get caught," Mac said.

"The *Sakinah* is the only lead we have," Brogan said as he finished his final equipment check, "and a solo visit is the only way to keep Amara alive."

"What if you don't show up at our meeting point?" Mac asked.

Brogan stopped. "I keep playing that nightmare in my head. Amara will die, and I probably will as well. Whatever happens, this operation must remain secret. You should just go home."

Adjusting his mask and mouthpiece, he slid noiselessly into Boston Harbor. No sound reached his ears as he slipped through the water. The odor of diesel oil mixed with the familiar smells of seaweed and fish. The sky was dark, and the water was cold, but the wet suit and his muscle activity made swimming tolerable. His decision not to use an oxygen tank and flippers seemed right.

The *Sakinah* lay three hundred yards away. Brogan followed a straight trajectory to its rudder. He saw two guards smoking under the halogen lights at the gangway, but no activity on the ship itself.

Reaching the *Sakinah's* stern, he hooked his left arm over the upper edge of the rudder. Stabilized, he used both hands to remove from his belt pack a claw-shaped hook attached to a length of thin high-strength Kevlar rope. He inserted the base of the hook into the barrel of a gas cartridge gun.

Face toward the sky, he now pushed off into the water and released the trigger, aiming for the ship's deck. A quiet puff, and the hook and line arced over the stern of the ship.

He pulled on the line and watched it fall back into the water. No attachment. He inserted another gas cartridge and repeated the maneuver. This time the claw held, and he scrambled up the line onto the rear deck, returning the hook and line to his belt pack.

He decided to investigate the control tower first, keeping low and in shadow. It was a five-story structure rising into the sky midway along the port side of the ship. As he ran along the periphery of the cargo hold on this crescent-mooned night, his dark face and wet suit would make him invisible. He could vaguely see the bays below him filled with containers ready to unload.

A light flashed from the gangway, accompanied by muffled voices, just as Brogan found the tower door. He opened it, and started to ascend, vowing not to use any light as he investigated the nerve center of the ship.

He activated his infrared goggles as he reached the first deck. He saw the green outlines of tables and a galley, smelled the cardamom, cumin, and turmeric aromas of past Moroccan cooking. The mess hall. No signs of human activity.

He ascended to the next level, opening the door into a large room containing hammocks. Here he identified a few sleeping sailors but did not disturb them. He repeated the same maneuvers on deck three. No evidence of a prisoner, although some berths had inhabitants. Some of the crew seemed to be on shore leave.

The final deck brought him to the bridge. The captain's quarters were locked. Two other wardrooms on that level were spacious but showed no signals of body heat.

As he finished his exploration, a light flashed from the container hold, blinking three times. Brogan moved toward the stairs to identify the source.

He startled to attack mode when his goggles suggested a heat source to his left. He ducked low and kicked out against his potential attacker, but his feet met only air. A whoosh was accompanied by a hot blur in his goggles. He turned. A ferocious blow to the head, and he felt consciousness slipping away.

Brogan shook his head to clear the fog. Darkness, and the stench of oil. Mouth packed with a cloth, dry and sore. Arms and legs tightly bound as he lay on a metal floor.

He could hear the slapping of waves, suggesting he was still on the ship. No other sound. *How long had it been since he was captured?* He heard footsteps approach, felt a burning in his left arm, then descended again into oblivion.

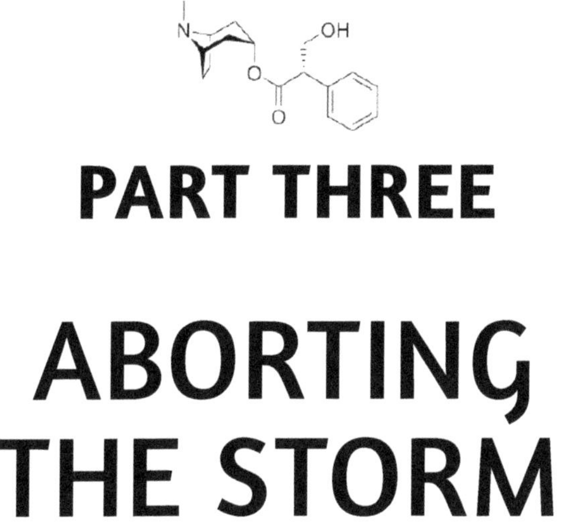

PART THREE

ABORTING THE STORM

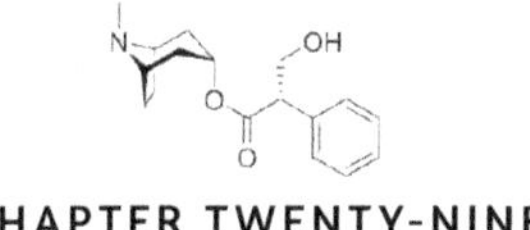

CHAPTER TWENTY-NINE

ON BOARD SAKINAH

BOSTON, MA
MAY 18-19, 2021

After Brogan entered the water, Mac drove his car around to the parking lot of Conley terminal and waited. By twelve-thirty, half an hour after Brogan had promised to return, Mac had received no news. He sat in the darkness debating whether to go to the police.

He realized that would be a death sentence for Brogan and Amara.

Should he then just go home and pretend nothing had happened, as Brogan had suggested?

He could not leave his friends. He spent half an hour studying a diagram of the innards of a container ship on his iPhone. He assumed he would never have to enter the lower deck containing engine room, ballast, and fuel tanks. He also did not plan to explore the cargo hold, which held the containers. The most likely place to find Brogan and Amara would be the bridge, which contained the helm, captain's and crew's quarters, mess, galley, lounges, and sick bay.

His watch showed one a.m. It was now or never for him to switch into rescue mode.

He crept in shadow from his car to the dock and observed the *Sakinah* from the cluster of trees at the edge of the pier. A youth dressed in a camo uniform with a rifle slung on one shoulder guarded the ship.

Mac wondered what special dispensation had allowed this ship to have an armed civilian guard, since Massachusetts had one of the most restrictive gun laws in the country. He extracted the pen/laser pointer he kept in his pocket for his lectures. Clicking the beam to *intermittent,* he propped the instrument on a tree branch next to him. He moved quickly away from the light toward the boat's gangway.

After a few minutes, the guard crossed to the trees, identified the source of the blinking, shook his head, and ran back toward the boat.

The guard's absence was all Mac needed to get on the ship. He slipped behind one of the mooring winches and watched the young man board, gun at the ready. As the youth crept past, Mac grabbed the rifle by the barrel and whipped it away. Before the boy could shout, Mac slid behind him and pulled the rifle barrel against his throat with all the strength of both arms. *Render him unconscious, don't kill him.* The youth slumped, unconscious.

Mac gagged and trussed the guard, then deposited him in a dark corner of the deck behind the anchor winch.

Next step: find Brogan and Amara. The search should start in the sick bay and crew's quarters. In the dim light of the crescent moon, Mac raced along the passageway above the deck. He reached the bridge entrance without difficulty, found the door unlocked, and mounted the first flight of stairs in semi-darkness. Signs on the first level confirmed it to be the galley and mess. He continued up the stairs to the next floor. Twenty bunks filled that space. Some of them contained sleeping sailors, but Mac saw no sign of a hostage or guard.

The third level should contain both bunks and sick bay. Mac glided silently along the narrow passageway between bunks, taking care not to waken any of the snoring sailors.

At the end of the passageway, he opened the door into what looked like the sick bay, with only a nightlight to illuminate it. He could make out that it contained two beds separated by a curtain, desk, inner door marked with a red cross, medicine cabinet, and sink.

A sudden blare of klaxons and lights transfixed him. *What the hell was going on?* He stared with terror at the berths he had just passed. Lights shone everywhere on the ship and the grinding noise of the alerting horns beggared thought. *Had he been discovered? Was this an intruder alarm?*

He entered the sick bay and closed the door behind him, straining to understand the words of the public address system. Arabic, French, and finally English crackled through the speaker system. "All personnel must now be on board. Everyone to be at assigned posts within ten minutes. Departure 0140 hours."

He checked his watch: 1:30 a.m.

The ship was supposed to remain in Boston for at least a day to unload Berserker powder and distribute it to the rest of the country. Instead, it would leave in ten minutes. Had

Brogan been captured? Was that the reason for the change in plan?

Mac's heart raced as he considered his next steps. He heard the rushing of feet and voices shouting in many languages outside his door. A cluster of sailors, but none apparently searching for him.

He locked the door and put his ear to it to understand better what they were saying. A confusion of tongues, but snatches of recognizable English. "Why did they call us back so quickly?" "Just starting with a beautiful bartender." "Where the hell are we going now?" Some of the words were slurred, suggesting their speaker had drunk a good deal.

A new voice spoke over the others, and the hubbub faded into silence. The speaker had a Brooklyn accent and seemed agitated. Mac recognized it as Steve Therman's voice. The silence when Therman spoke suggested he was the leader of the crew.

"You will have to sober up fast, men. An emergency forced us to change plans. We leave in five minutes, and everyone is expected to carry out assigned duties as scheduled. Any questions, my colleague Jane will take care of them just like she usually does."

Silence, then one man spoke up. Mac could hear him easily through the closed door.

"No woman tells me what to do," the voice said with a heavy Russian accent. "Not doing anything more tonight. Need sleep. Besides, drunk."

A response from a woman—must be Jane—that Mac could not hear clearly.

"Sure you will. You and twenty other bitches," the Russian voice said.

Sounds of the smack of a fist into the gut and a body hitting the floor. A man howling in pain, then silence.

A cacophony of excited voices. "Did you see that?" "Out like a light…bare hands."

The boat began to move.

The woman's voice again. "Your friend Boris needs a place to sober up and think about his future. What's behind this door?"

"Sick bay."

"Perfect," Jane answered. "If he's not sick now, he's going to be. And if he doesn't smarten up, he might end up dead."

Mac heard footsteps and the sound of a man being dragged toward him. He had to get out of the way fast, looked around for some place to become invisible.

"The door's locked," a voice said from the other side of the door.

"No problem," Jane answered. "I can open this kind of lock easily. Just hold Boris's feet for me."

Desperate to hide, Mac moved to the door marked with a red cross and opened it to find a small inner office with a toilet, sink, medicine cabinet, desk, and closet. It appeared to be the medic's personal space. Mac yanked open the closet door and found white coats and scrubs hanging. He could barely fit behind them as he closed the door from inside.

He heard the scraping sounds of a lock being picked, then the door to the outer office opening.

"This'll be a good place for him to sober up," Jane said. "Is there a corpsman on the ship?"

"What's corpsman?" a voice asked.

"Someone who knows about medicine."

"Nobody like that. We all use sick bay if feeling bad."

"You'll have to keep an eye on Boris in this space overnight. Lucky for him he's a good engineer when he's sober. I'd dump him overboard otherwise."

"Yes sir, I mean ma'am," the male voice said.

"What's behind the door with the red cross?"

"The medical office."

"Does it have a head?"

"Yes."

"I'll be back in a minute."

Mac heard the door open, toilet flush, and a woman's steps directed toward his closet. He heard her ask, "What's this?"

Mac held his breath, tried to fold his thin six-foot frame behind the coats. But the shoes — nothing would conceal his shoes. He debated whether to rush her if she opened the door.

"Jane, I need you. Boris is puking." The voice from the outside room was urgent.

Jane's steps moved away. A few minutes later unsteady footfalls and many curses accompanied the smell of vomit as Boris and Jane entered the bathroom. The sound of retching and toilet flushing filled the air.

Jane's voice issued from the space just outside Mac's closet. "Vladimir, I hold you responsible if anything keeps this man from doing his job tomorrow at dawn."

A door clanked closed.

The voices receded. Mac opened the closet door enough to let air in but realized quickly the vomit had not all been cleaned up. He closed the door again.

He checked his watch's luminescent dial. Two a.m.

He waited half an hour, then crept to the door leading to the sick bay and opened it a crack. Boris lay on one of the beds, snoring loudly. His friend Vladimir sat on a chair beside him, very much awake, working on his smartphone.

Mac had no choice but to wait as well. He turned back into the medical office and found a chair in the dark.

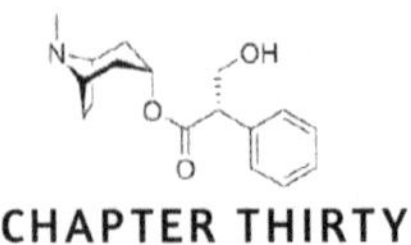

CHAPTER THIRTY

MAC'S DISCOVERIES

ON BOARD SAKINAH
MAY 19, 2021

After another hour, Mac opened the door to the sick bay and looked at the beds. Boris continued to snore, but his companion Vladimir had left.

Mac put on a white coat and headed into the sick bay. *Could he get by the snoring drunk? Would the white coat protect him or target him?*

"Hey Doc! Can I go back to engineering deck now?" Boris' voice seemed extra loud in the room as Mac tried to escape.

Heart pounding, Mac took on the role of ship's doctor. "Are you sure you're ready?"

"Of course. This isn't first time I drank too much. You new?"

"Just got added for this trip," Mac replied.

"Great. Give support to get back to proper place."

Mac considered his options. Leading Boris back to the engine room would provide him an opportunity to continue his search for Amara and Brogan but would also expose him to discovery.

He decided to take his chances.

"OK," Mac said. "Just lean on me."

With Boris shuffling and swaying, the duo passed through the dormitory of sailors with a few taunts but no serious obstructions.

A sentry guarded the departure from the bridge. Boris took the initiative. "This is doctor who escort me back to engineering deck."

The guard stared at Mac. "I've never seen you on the ship before."

"Just got recruited by Therman."

The guard started for his phone, but Boris lurched toward him and the man drew away with an expression of disgust.

"Get him out of here. Be sure he doesn't throw up on you."

"I'll do my best," Mac said as they passed by.

When they got to the engine room, Boris thanked Mac with an outpouring of bad breath and alcohol. "Can't stand sick bay. Smells like disinfectant. I miss engines' noise. Part of blood now. You understand?" He slumped into a cot beside the turbines and before Mac could respond, began to snore.

Mac looked around the room. No other people in sight. He took the stairs up the deck to the dark night.

The Atlantic breeze had become a stiff wind, and the ocean swells lifted and dropped the ship despite its size. A quarter moon lit the sky along with a million stars, and the waves foamed as they pounded the bow. The ship was semi-lit with running lights. No one appeared to be wandering about the decks. Mac estimated they were somewhere on the Atlantic about an hour southeast of Boston. He could continue his search for Brogan and Amara unimpeded.

In the dim light, Mac could make out the silhouettes of containers in the cargo hold. They were not all piled on each other. Twenty individual containers formed a cluster like a small village. Stacked units surrounded them.

A single path led to the container settlement, with internal corridors creating a maze barely visible from the gangway. Mac descended the sturdy metal stairway to the cargo hold, easily identifying the entrance to the central settlement. Voices in a foreign language echoed in the semi-lit area at the beginning of the maze. He picked up a rifle leaning against the wall of the complex.

Approaching footsteps and the acrid smell of strong cigarette smoke pushed Mac into the shadow of the nearest container. He flattened against the wall, holding his breath as a guard with an assault rifle marched by and stopped. The tip of the cigarette in the man's mouth glowed red in the pitch-black night.

Mac shrank back. *Why had the guard stopped? Had he sensed Mac's presence?*

After a few long seconds, the man continued up the stairs.

Mac waited until the footsteps disappeared before he moved into the low lighting of the central area and retraced the man's path. Again, the smell of strong tobacco filled his nostrils.

Mac tracked the scent past three containers. The olfactory trail stopped at a container in the center of the settlement. Its door was ajar, and Mac could see a cigarette tip glowing in the opening.

"Can I borrow a cigarette?" Mac asked in English, standing outside the door frame and holding his rifle by the barrel.

The guard swung the door open and stepped out to see who had spoken. Mac swung at the red cigarette tip with the butt of the rifle. A crack of bone, and the body crumpled.

Mac dragged the guard back into the room, closed the door behind them, and flicked on his cell phone light. He was in an anteroom, ten feet deep, with a closed door in the wall before him. The stench of cigarette smoke filled the air. A chair was its sole piece of furniture.

Taking the combat knife from the unconscious guard's belt, Mac sliced strips of fabric from the man's shirt, trussed and gagged him, and hauled him into a corner. He moved to the inner door, where the first three keys on the guard's ring did nothing. The fourth turned in the lock and the entryway burst open.

The space was pitch black, smelling of urine and sweat. The cell phone light showed it to be about the same size as the antechamber.

A figure lay unmoving on a mat on the floor.

Mac knelt at the prisoner's side. A Black male, stripped down to his shorts. Blindfold, mouth gag, duct tape restraints. Mac ripped off the blindfold and pulled out the gag, then slashed the duct tape to release arms and legs.

Brogan.

A sedated Brogan whose limbs flopped when lifted and whose eyes remained closed.

A half-filled syringe and bottle labelled sodium thiopental sat on a table beside the bed.

Mac would not be able to do anything with his CIA friend until the sedation wore off. He pulled the mattress with Brogan on it out to the antechamber, dragged the guard to replace it in the cell, and emptied the syringe contents into the guard's jugular vein. He locked the inner door, pocketed the keys, and left Brogan in the antechamber to be picked up later.

Amara still had to be found.

Mac examined the corridors around the container he had entered. Three containers away, a folding chair lay against the wall. Mac knocked, his rifle again held by the barrel.

"Omar?" the voice asked. Mac gave no response.

The door opened and the guard appeared, shouting in Arabic. Mac swatted the man's head with such force that he could hear skull bones reposition. Dragging him into the room and locking the door, Mac surveyed the space with pounding heart.

His phone beam showed an operating room light and dentist chair in the center of this antechamber with an instrument tray beside it—a setup for torture. Was this the container that held Amara?

The arrangement seemed otherwise the same as Brogan's container, with a door leading to an inner chamber. Mac moved to the lock, clutching the keys he had taken from the guard.

This time the first key opened the door.

Inside the room, he could smell vomit but see nothing. He felt for a light switch beside the door, flicked it on, and was blinded by the light. With semi-closed eyes, he surveyed the space. A toilet in one corner, a sink, a chair, and a bed. A body chained to the bed.

It was Amara. Her face was pale, streaked with dirt and

crossed by matted strands of hair. An ankle chain bound her to the bed. A stained dress covered her body. Grime stained her bare feet. He tried all the rest of the keys on the guard's chain and found none of them unlocked her restraint. But her eyes opened as he lifted her chin to look at her.

"Mac," she said in a croaking voice, "I knew you would come."

"Amara, what have they done to you?"

"More than I can bear." Her voice was a whisper, and tears dripped onto her cheeks. "They're going to kill me next."

"Not if I can help it." Mac's heart thumped.

"They'll lock me in a cage with berserker monkeys—the kind that murdered Khaled," Amara mumbled so softly Mac could hardly hear her.

The image of the dead Interpol agent he autopsied in Tangier flashed into Mac's mind.

"What cage? Where is it?"

"Next to this container, I think. Close by."

"What else does the ship carry?"

"Everything they need." Her eyes closed.

"Amara, please stay awake. I need to know what I'm dealing with. What is 'everything'?"

"Everything to manufacture, test, and distribute Berserker." She seemed exhausted by the effort of the long sentence.

"How do you know?" Mac realized Amara was making a great effort to stay focused.

"They talk about it while they're torturing me."

"Who are they? Who's the leader"

"Therman. Now there's a woman too. Jane."

"My God, Amara. I'm so sorry," Mac said.

Amara grabbed his shirt with both hands and looked at him with wide eyes, energized. "Mac, you've got to get us out of here."

"I will, I promise. Do you know where we're headed?"

"New Jersey was what they were talking about. They planned to distribute the drug from Boston but freaked when they discovered an intruder on board." Amara's head drooped again.

"Do you know who has the key to your ankle chain? Is it Therman or the woman?"

"Therman."

"I'll be back to release you." Mac started for the door.

"Be careful." Amara mumbled as she fell back onto the bed.

Mac exited and moved to the container next door, finding the appropriate entry key among those he had taken from the guard.

The overpowering odor of animal fur and excrement assaulted him as he stepped into the room. He flicked a switch beside the door, flooding the space with light.

A dozen macaques climbed, jumped, and rattled the bars of a large cage in the center of the room, grunting, jabbering, contorting their faces at the new arrival. Occasionally they took water from a trough leading to a tank outside the cage.

Several bottles of powder sat beside the tank. One bottle sported the label "Berserker." The monkey embedded in the

Moroccan's neck, the disastrous Carnival in Rio, the maddened crowd at the Louvre, all flashed through Mac's mind. *Was this powder the common denominator for those events?*

Mac found an empty bottle on the medicine shelf and poured the Berserker powder into it, closing its cap tightly before he stuffed it into his pocket. He poured sugar taken the from shelf into the bottle marked Berserker. If Therman did want to kill Amara with violent monkeys, the powder would be inactive.

Next, he had to find Therman to get the keys to Amara's ankle restraints. The control tower would be the most likely place to look.

He climbed to the tower and ascended the steps toward the galley.

A large tank outside the mess hall marked "Drinking water" caught his attention. He paused as he passed it. What if he spiked the water supply with Berserker? In the ship's drinking water, the drug would affect crewmen as they recovered from their leave. The resulting chaos might produce enough disorder to allow him, Amara, and Brogan to get off the ship, or at least buy them time to be rescued.

But might also cause violent death among members of the crew. Could he justify such slaughter?

Amara, Brogan, and he would surely be killed if they were found. And if the distribution of the Berserker powder was not stopped now, thousands or even millions of innocent Americans could die.

Mac poured all the Berserker powder into the drinking water.

He continued his search for the keys to Amara's chains. Outside the captain's quarters, there was no sign of Therman or the woman named Jane. Mac did hear the captain and first mate complain about the order to leave Boston precipitously, without a tugboat or other accompaniment. They cursed that it might end their careers.

"But it's better than being shot by that crazy Therman," one said.

"Or his even crazier Lady Jane," the other agreed.

"Thank God they're not interfering with us on the bridge."

Realizing he would not find Therman in the tower, Mac hustled down the stairway and back to Amara's container. Perhaps he could find another way to release her chains.

Everything seemed as he left it. He opened the door to the chamber and approached to tell her what he had done.

He felt a crushing blow to his head.

Mac had no idea what day it was. The place was hot and smelled of mold. His shirt stuck to his body and his pants were soaked with sweat. His head hurt. He could hardly breathe through the gag that covered his mouth.

He heard the clanking of an opening door. "Dr. MacGregor, I presume." An American man with a Brooklyn accent. Short, silhouetted in the light that filtered through the door. The man strode toward him, withdrew the gag, looked at him with unblinking gaze.

"And you are?" Mac asked, pain wracking his throat as he talked.

"Steven Therman. You may think I will be interrogating

you to find out what you were doing snooping around my ship. Don't worry. I won't, because I don't care. It's far beyond that."

"Amara?"

Therman laughed. "Amara Zadi. Is anyone safe in these days of terrorism and international unrest?"

Looking at Mac with narrowed eyelids, he said. "She's as safe as you are. I've enjoyed our little discussion." He moved directly beside Mac and injected Mac's thigh with a material that burned.

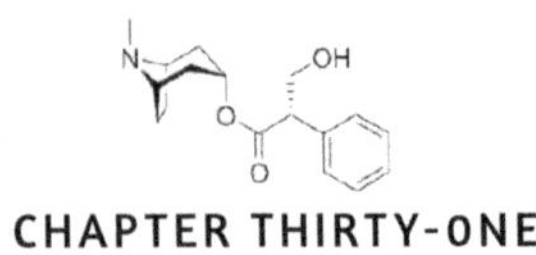

CHAPTER THIRTY-ONE

BERSERKER CHAOS

ON BOARD SAKINAH
MAY 19, 2021

Groggy and dazed, Mac began to wake up. The stench of feces and animal fur made his stomach churn. He felt a paw touching his cheek, wiped a splatter of something from his forehead.

He forced his eyes open. The forehead splatter was stool. Simian eyes glared at him from a few inches distance. Their owner extended an arm to explore his face. A dozen other macaques stared, some close, some farther away. The animals chattered, pointed, retreated, flung food and feces at each other and at the wall.

Surveying the situation by turning his head, Mac realized the full extent of his predicament. He lay propped up against one wall of a large monkey enclosure, arms and legs trussed with zip-ties. Amara, still heavily drugged, lay shackled to his left. Brogan, also semi-comatose, lay to his right. Neither would be functional in time to help with any plan.

The grating of the door to the room drew his attention away from his friends. Therman walked through the doorway and stood beside the water bottle hanging on the cage. "Nice to see you awake, MacGregor," he said. "You'll be able

186

to appreciate what's about to happen. Too bad your friends are too doped up to care."

Therman picked up the bottle of white powder marked Berserker from a shelf and emptied it into the monkeys' water supply. Mac recognized it as the bottle he had filled with sugar powder. "Normally we only use a few tablespoons," Therman continued, "but I want to be sure we get the full effect for you and your friends." He checked his watch. "Usually takes twenty minutes." He slammed the door behind him as he left the room.

Mac tried to think about how to escape but could not get his thoughts together. It was like trying to move his mind through quicksand. He felt cloudy, unfocused, desperately wanting to fall back into oblivion. He contemplated how drugs can change the nervous system, but it did not help.

A well-placed lump of stool hitting his chest made him realize there was a problem even if the monkeys did not go berserk.

Therman came back and placed himself outside the cage just behind Mac. As he talked, he fingered a sac slung around one shoulder. "The twenty minutes are up," he said in a loud whisper in Mac's ear. "You won't last long when the party begins. But before you die, I want to introduce you to my associate Jane. She's a big part of the reason you're where you are right now. And together we're going to change the world. Without your interference."

He stepped aside to reveal a woman in her thirties, fit and beautiful, but with dark eyes that made Mac's blood run cold.

"And now let the games begin," Therman said with a smile.

Mac leaned back, unable to focus his mind.

Therman and Jane continued to wait with increasingly puzzled expressions. The monkeys pointed and chittered but did not attack. Finally, Therman turned toward the exit. "I need to talk to—"

A crush of sailors blasted through the door before he could move. At their head was a man in Saudi robes, who snarled as he raced to Therman. "I thought I would find you here, you bastard," he shouted. "I've been doing your shit jobs for three years now, and I'm finished."

Mac rolled away from the wall of the cage onto his side to watch. Whatever was happening, it was not what Therman had intended.

"Hameni, my brother, you have always been my right hand," Therman said as he put out his arms to greet the Arab. "I relied on you to set up the Berserker manufacturing and testing. How can you—?"

Hameni forced Therman back against the cage. He inserted something into Therman's gut; Mac realized in a moment it was a very long knife. Hameni sliced upward and intestines spilled out of Therman's abdominal wall. Blood and fluid from the wound sprayed Mac.

Jane ripped the pouch from Therman's shoulder and disappeared.

Therman slid down the outside wall of the cage, trying to turn away from his attacker. The hemorrhage continued, blood covering the floor. In a few seconds, he was dead, knife still protruding from his abdominal wall.

Hameni did not have time to enjoy his triumph. A tall sailor behind him grabbed his head and twisted with a violent jerk. Hameni stopped breathing in mid-gasp and fell limp to the floor.

Four men wielding cudgels and fire axes pounced on the muscular sailor and each other. One of them rattled the cage Mac and the others were lying in. Mac watched the man's ferocious expression freeze as his skull split from top to bottom, cleaved by a colleague with an ax. Blood, brain, and spinal fluid spattered over Mac and everything in the cage.

One assailant grabbed his head and collapsed without any apparent provocation, falling lifeless onto the floor. Others continuted to attack each other.

The monkeys in the cage jabbered, jumped, and squealed as they saw the mayhem around them. Within twenty minutes, all the men who had poured through the door lay lifeless on the floor, torn apart and murdered by each other.

Now fully alert, Mac watched horror-stricken. The men must have drunk the Berserker powder he had put in the ship's water. He shuddered at the devastation that would happen if the tons of powder from the ship's containers were added to the water supply of American cities.

But there was a more pressing problem right now—the monkeys in the cage. No longer playful, they seemed upset by the carnage around them. They poked more aggressively and made louder noises. One older male pushed his finger against Mac's chest. Mac began to fear for his safety in the cage, even though it had protected them from the berserk sailors outside.

He could feel his strength and energy return. The knife blade still protruded from Therman's slit abdomen, touching the cage. Mac could just reach the hilt through the bars. He pulled. Nothing happened; Hameni had embedded the weapon well. Mac pulled again. Sweat mingled with the spattered blood on his brow, dripping into his eyes. He grunted with exertion. The monkeys clustered around him.

Mac staggered to his feet, bent over to grab the knife and use the leverage of his body to extract it. It yielded, almost sending him to the floor, but came free in his hands. He now had a way of removing his restraints.

Cutting the leg ties was easy, but the hand zip-ties were more difficult. He finally maneuvered the knife so it would cut the wrist ropes. He moved quickly back to Amara and Brogan, cut their bonds, and realized they would be incapacitated for a long time as they flopped onto the floor of the cage, breathing heavily.

Mac sat exhausted, covered in blood and body fluids, trying to make sense of what just happened. Had the entire crew been affected by the drug? Would others still try to kill him if he ventured outside?

He moved to Therman's body and retrieved a revolver and keys to the cage. He opened the cage door and lay back with the gun in his hand, waiting.

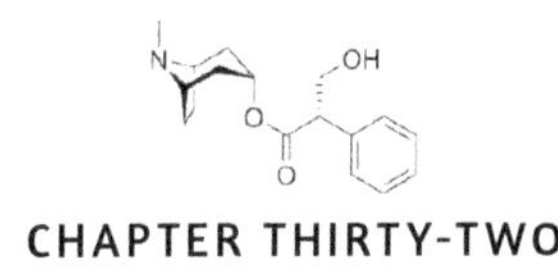

CHAPTER THIRTY-TWO

MAC AT HOME

The events that followed on the *Sakinah* were a blur. Mac chalked it up to the Pentothal still circulating in his system. He remembered Brogan disappearing, and returning to say he had summoned the Coast Guard. He said everyone else was dead, helped Mac and Amara to the deck.

Mac could not forget the whining of helicopter blades coming to a stop on the deck, the dozens of special agents swarming over the ship. He definitely remembered their removing Amara with Brogan's reassurance that she would be returned to her father safely.

After that, he wasn't sure of anything. He was taken to a regional hospital and released later that day, feeling clear about the present but still cloudy about the past.

He tried to call Lauren but got no answer, finally deciding just to go to his house. It had been less than forty-eight hours since he had left, though it felt longer. Brogan drove him home, delivering him to the front door. "How can I thank you?" he asked as Mac headed in.

Mac barely heard him, looking forward to an enthusiastic greeting when he walked into the house. He realized how much his family anchored him, often counterbalancing the distress he had to deal with in his life.

Silence and an empty house greeted him.

He checked his watch. Seven. Not terribly late for dinner.

A note in Maggie's handwriting sat on the kitchen table. "Dear Daddy, where are you? We have to go." An addendum in Lauren's script added. "At the school auditorium for oral presentation evening. Did you forget?"

Mac changed clothes and drove through the labyrinth of streets to the school, where he now remembered both Maggie and Peter had been chosen to give brief talks as part of an initiative to teach children public speaking.

He found a parking place easily, probably because some parents had already left. He hoped the evening started with the youngest students first, then moved to the older classes. That way, he would at least be on time to hear his own children's presentations.

The auditorium was full of masked parents and siblings. He knew the omicron variant of COVID had reached Massachusetts, although it had produced no devastation like that in Florida, Mississippi, or Texas. Most Massachusetts residents were vaccinated, and all wore masks without complaint.

Mac stood at the back of the auditorium, surveying the crowd to identify Lauren. There was no social distancing in the seating, and most chairs were occupied. He walked down the left side aisle while he scanned the program and the audience. He heard Peter's name announced as he got to the front row, slid into a chair vacated by a previous parent, and waited for his eight-year-old son to begin.

Peter stepped onto the stage. "My topic will be the Vikings." He seemed to lose energy, looking over the assembly while the attendees waited in silence. His eyes lighted on Mac, and his sad expression broke into a toothy smile. Mac smiled back, gave him a thumbs up sign, and looked around again for Lauren.

Peter described the early Viking raids including Lindisfarne. He paused, outlined the use of drugs to enhance the Viking's performance, then continued in almost a conspiratorial tone. "But modern research has revealed something the Vikings never knew. There is a special gene in inhabitants of Norway, Sweden, and Scotland"—he winked at Mac—"that metabolizes the drug that made Viking warriors go wild. If you have that gene, you just become a strong warrior. If you don't have the gene, your brain blows up and you die when you take the drug."

He stopped and looked at Mac. "This scientific research just happened this year. I know because my dad helped discover it. You better be a real Viking if you take the magic potion. Otherwise, watch out!"

The audience applauded vigorously. Peter looked at Mac with a grin.

Mac followed his son's subsequent gaze to find Lauren, who sat on the opposite side of the auditorium almost on the aisle. Waiting until the next student finished her talk, Mac moved to a spot in the row behind his wife. She did not turn to acknowledge him, appeared deliberately to stare straight ahead. His stomach sank. He had some explaining to do.

Maggie's turn to perform came twenty minutes later. She chose Tennyson's poem *Ulysses,* one of Mac's favorites. "I am a part of all that I have met, and all experience is an arch wherethrough gleams that untravell'd world…" Mac felt his heart skip. *What magic had bestowed the blessing of such children?* He led the applause when Maggie finished. Ten minutes later the evening concluded, and the audience began to disperse.

He slipped into a now-vacant seat beside his wife. "Sorry to be late," he said. "I did catch both kids' performances."

"A half hour later and you would have missed the whole thing," Lauren said.

"I'm sorry. I just lost sense of the time. I was involved in governmental stuff."

"All I know is you weren't there to help Maggie and Peter get ready for their performances," Lauren continued, speaking in an undertone but very forcefully. "They were both convinced you were going to miss the event completely. I texted you, but you didn't even acknowledge my text. We have to talk when we get home."

Peter and Maggie seemed beyond excited when they appeared several minutes later.

"Did you like my science?" Peter said. "I had to mention you because they might not have believed me otherwise."

"Isn't that a great poem?" Maggie said. "I love the part about not yielding at the end."

"You were both wonderful," Mac said. "Your mother and I were so proud of you, weren't we, Lauren?" Lauren smiled, but Mac knew there was more to come.

On the way home, the conversation was led by the children—the nerves they had experienced behind the scenes, their decision to do what they did, what the other kids said about their performances.

"I don't want to go to sleep," Maggie said. "I just want to think about the next time I'm on stage."

"Will that be next year?" Mac asked.

"No, they'll do tryouts in the fall just like they did last month. The next show will be to celebrate Thanksgiving."

"What about you, Peter? Will you want to give another talk?"

"Maybe," Peter said. "I want to find out more about that special powder—you know, the one that made some of the Vikings berserk."

"Good luck with that," Mac said. "I have a friend named Dr. Wu who might help."

Lauren and Mac finally got the children to bed and were able to sit quietly in the conservatory, surrounded by orange trees, roses, and other flowering plants.

"I'm worried about where your international work is taking you," Lauren began. "Dabbling in stuff outside the hospital is a big problem. It suggests you care more about travelling around the world than you do about the day-to-day work that pays our bills. If I tried to list your priorities, I would put your international work first, the patient care at the hospital next, the family and me third, research fourth, and teaching fifth. Not a good place for a wife to be on the priority list."

"Lauren, that's not fair. I always try to keep you front and center."

"Like missing tonight's performances?" Her voice rose a

decibel. "It left me high and dry, not front and center. I had no idea what to say to the children when they feared you would not show up. There's only a certain amount of damage control I can do."

"I promise to do better."

"That's what you always say, Mac, but where is the action that supports it?"

Mac thought about the Independence Day holiday coming up. "What about July fourth? Would you let me make it a family event? I know some people who would let us watch the fireworks from a great vantage point."

"I don't know, Mac. It might be reasonable if we don't have to sit on the esplanade with five hundred thousand of our closest friends spending the evening crowded on the riverbank. Could you really make it possible to watch the fireworks without the hassle?"

"I think I can arrange something where we don't have to mingle with the crowds. We'll be in a rooftop on the Cambridge side of the Charles, just up the river from the fireworks.

"Maybe that would work," Lauren said. "If it doesn't get messed up some way."

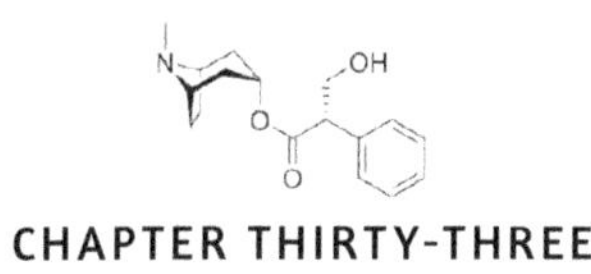

CHAPTER THIRTY-THREE

JANE ESCAPES

Watching the evolving chaos around her on the ship, Jane realized the crew of the *Sakinah* must have ingested the Berserker compound. She had no interest in finding out how, or becoming part of their mutual destruction. She had to abandon ship.

Folding Therman's pouch under her arm and holding a knife in her hand, she raced toward the bridge like a running back heading for the end zone. Twisting, weaving, side-stepping crew members as they chopped at each other with knives and axes, she reached the bridge unscathed.

Her target was the rescue boat, a twelve-foot open-cockpit vessel suspended over the water on a davit. In case of an emergency, this boat was kept ready for immediate deployment with an outboard motor primed and filled with gas. After pulling the quick-release mechanism that lowered the vessel into the ocean, Jane turned to face a gang of crewmen.

"Get her," the man in the lead shouted. Six men raced toward her. As they closed in, she drove her knife into the leader, pushed him back against the others, and jumped into the Atlantic.

Treading water, she could see the men trying to raise the boat again. Their interference unclamped it from its davits and it fell bow first into the sea. Its pontoons allowed it to right itself quickly.

Jane scrambled aboard, watching the *Sakinah* move away with its forward momentum.

Two men hurled themselves from the deck into the water to pursue Jane. Balancing in the wave-tossed boat, she grabbed an oar and waited for the first man to surface. As his head lifted above the water, she swung the oar full force, hitting him with the thin edge of the blade on the side of the scalp. The sound of splintering bone was followed by a gasp. The man sank beneath the waves.

The second sailor approached from the stern, staying low in the water to avoid the oar. As he lifted himself out of the water by grabbing onto the outboard motor, Jane started the motor and the propellors roared to life, frothing the water. The man screamed, dropped off the boat, and bobbed in the center of a widening blood stain. As he floated upright, Jane could see that the propellors had removed his feet, replacing them with stumps of leg that would bleed him to death in minutes.

Shouts and a few scattered shots from the disappearing *Sakinah*'s deck did nothing to impede her escape now. Within seconds she was out of range of pursuit. As she aimed her skiff toward the Long Island shore, Jane saw two Coast Guard helicopters racing above her to the *Sakinah*'s last location.

She found a cove on the shore covered with trees and pulled the boat under it. Once safely on the shore, she checked that her own money belt was intact with credit cards, IDs, and cash. Her attention turned to Therman's pouch hanging from her shoulder. With a combat knife, she ripped it open and examined its contents: a bag of Berserker powder, enough to make a thousand people berserk and serve as template for manufacturing more; a thumb drive whose contents she would explore later; a letter from Rufus Morlock to Therman saying Morlock held the right to change plans at will; four passports and IDs with different names but all with Therman's picture; several bank cards and credit cards, and a large envelope filled with hundred-dollar bills.

Jane would be financially OK, but her Sicilian blood boiled. *How had her plan been thwarted?* Someone was to blame for this. Of course, Duncan MacGregor was one culprit, and she would get to him. But there was another person she needed to exact retribution from, a man who had hidden in the shadows too long, a manipulator and user.

In the Sicilian town of Corleone where her family originated, Jane learned the world could be divided into family and non-family. Family privileges extended to colleagues like her fellow soldiers in Afghanistan. Non-family included everyone else, but within that class were a subgroup considered enemies. When her family moved to the Bronx, the concept that enemies must be eliminated, and insults redressed, remained central in her thinking.

MacGregor was an enemy. She would kill him and his family. But first, she had a larger reckoning. Rufus Morlock, the master funder and designer of the whole disastrous affair, had left her and her colleagues flailing in the wind. She would not forgive. She would destroy him.

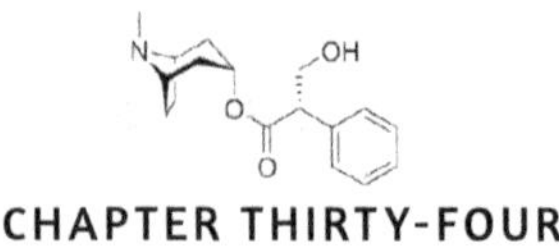

CHAPTER THIRTY-FOUR

MORLOCK ON MONTAUK

MONTAUK, LONG ISLAND
MAY 20, 2021

Morlock loved his Montauk retreat home even more than his Sixth Avenue penthouse. In Manhattan, he could feel the power of the media empire he had built. The process had started simply—a few radio stations and newspapers to try to give an alternative to institutional newspapers. Forced out of New Zealand, he came to the United States and added a sports network. It succeeded beyond anything he could hope, both as a source of revenue and as a hook to catch everyday Americans in his disinformation network.

He could leave all that behind on his Montauk beach estate. His house was not as magnificent as some Long Island Gatsby mansions, but his seashore was beyond compare. Every day he stayed on Long Island he did a morning beach walk, often imagining he was a Viking who had just made the sea voyage across the Atlantic.

The news of the *Sakinah*'s capture and the slaughter on board had angered him. He had little concern that he would be implicated in any way in the disaster. Many shell companies lay between him and the Moroccan ownership. He was relieved to be rid of Therman, who had too much ambition

200

and too few street smarts. The only downside was the loss of men and manufacturing capacity for the Berserker powder. No real problem with those items. Both men and machine were replaceable. He remained the power behind the scenes.

An early morning spring mist made this morning magic. He and his Cavalier King Charles spaniel had the beach to themselves. All entrances to his estate were carefully guarded and everyone in the neighborhood knew not to trespass on his shoreline. He gave himself to complete enjoyment of the morning—the fine sand crunching under his bare feet, the scent of fresh ocean air and occasional beach roses, lazy ocean surf washing in and out, eight a.m. fog reluctantly yielding to the rising sun, and the knowledge of complete security.

The appearance of a jogger disturbed his calm. She was a striking thirty-something woman, tall for a girl, toned but not too muscular, with short dark hair and large performer sunglasses almost hiding her face. Her bikini was revealing but not improper, with a soft belt at her waist. She ran in bare feet at the edge of the sea.

She was the kind of girl he would have bedded with delight two decades ago. At seventy, he found the juices flowing much slower than they once did. Pity.

As she reached speaking range, he called out "I'm sorry, this is a private beach."

She stopped six feet from him. "I had no idea. Whose property is it?"

"Really not your business. I must ask you to leave."

She moved to the spaniel, squatted and petted him as

he put his front paws on her, tail wagging. "Wonderful dog. Thoroughbred King Charles, right? What's his name?"

"Tamburlaine. But really, you must leave my property."

"Wait, are you Rufus Morlock? The incomparable Rufus Morlock? Is this your place?"

He could not help but smile. Although he tried to avoid publicity, he was flattered when attractive young women recognized him. Perhaps he would consider a fling with this female after all, some time.

"And if I am, and it is?"

"Then I have something for you."

She took off her soft belt. Murtaugh thought she was going to take out a phone and ask for a selfie with him.

She moved closer to him.

"What do you have?" he asked with mild curiosity.

"A gift from Steve Therman," she whispered.

Morlock's pleasant morning turned to dust. His heart pounded and he turned to run, but the woman tripped him and lunged on top of him as he fell face down in the sand. His glasses flew off. Before he could reach for them, she flipped him on his back and pounced to kneel on his chest and hold him down.

"What the hell are you doing?" he tried to shout as he thrashed to dislodge her. His voice faded as she stuffed her soft belt into his mouth. "I can make you very rich," he croaked as the last passages of his throat were closed off.

He thrashed and twisted to grab the woman who was about to take his life. "The way you made Therman and all those sailors on the *Sakinah* rich? No thanks," were the last words she said to him. Breathing became impossible and darkness enveloped him.

Jane held Morlock's mouth closed until he had stopped breathing for ten minutes by her watch. He did not move when she climbed off him. His arms flopped like a rag doll's when she lifted them, and he stared unblinking at the sky. He was completely and irretrievably dead.

She pulled the soft belt out of his throat. No lacerations or abrasions she could identify. No one will consider this a murder.

The dog continued to cavort and rub against her leg.

Putting on plastic gloves taken from her belt, she brushed away the sand from Morlock's face, leaving the spectacles where they had fallen. She arranged the body as if he had collapsed with a sudden cardiac arrest. She had been careful to run in the wet sand, and the rising tide was already obliterating her footprints. Within an hour, water would reach the dead body and perhaps carry it out to sea.

The King Charles spaniel still stood over Morlock's body, licking the side of his face.

Jane jogged back along the water edge in the direction she had come from, letting the waves wash over her feet. She had seen no one on her jog to Morlock's beach and no one as she left. By the time the body was found, she would be far away.

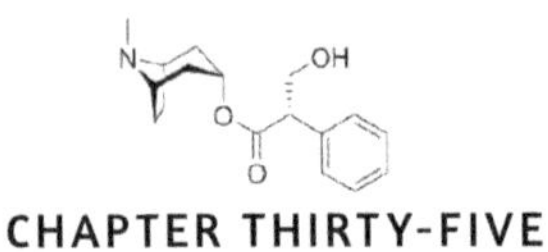

CHAPTER THIRTY-FIVE

SEARCH COMMITTEE MEETING SIX

HARBOR HOSPITAL, BOSTON, MA
MAY 21, 2021

Max Eli prepared to welcome the search committee to his neurology department conference room. Although it was the sixth meeting of the committee to recommend a chair for the about-to-be-created department of neurosurgery, it was their first in-person gathering.

He surveyed the space, redolent with history. The carpet, oak conference table, crimson leather chairs, and glassed-in bookcases set the tone. The portraits of previous luminaries, all distinguished white men, established that this was a department of substance.

Seeing the twelve committee members around one table made him realize how well he had engineered the composition of the group. Despite the tendency to require minorities on such committees, he had stuck to the formula that had made the hospital so successful in the past. Two Black women, including the obligatory representative from the medical school, were the only exceptions.

"Wonderful to see you all for our first face-to-face gathering," Eli began. "Unfortunately, Dr. Julia Pedroza is doing an emergency operation and will not be able to join us." He hoped he sounded disappointed but was secretly delighted. Pedroza's absence would remove a major barrier to his plan. He really did want to stop MacGregor from being the chair of the new neurosurgery department. Nothing personal, just preparing the way for his own ascendancy to power in the neuroscience institute to come.

"Today we will finalize our recommendations for the chief of the department of neurosurgery to be submitted to the hospital CEO," Eli continued. "Our finalists—Dr. Kenneth Kalangi from the University of California San Diego, Dr. Rose Ellen Merrek from the University of Nebraska, and Dr. Duncan MacGregor from our own institution—have all agreed to serve if selected."

James Welsh, a member of the department of neurology, gestured to be recognized. Eli smiled as he acknowledged his colleague. The interruption had been prearranged.

"Mr. Chairman," Welsh said, "we should also consider one other candidate—Dr. John Herman. Dr. Herman trained here eight years ago and has subsequently done excellent work at the University of West Texas, where he has become Chair of Neurosurgery."

Eli tried to make his look of surprise seem genuine, as if he and Welsh had not planned everything that was going to happen now. Eli would ask Welsh the reasons to propose Herman's name. Welsh would say that trainees and staff at Harbor Hospital enjoyed working with Herman, who had risen to be the chief unusually quickly in Texas. Recruited back to Harbor Hospital, the Texan would provide young energetic leadership for a young energetic department. He had already committed to do whatever Eli wanted as a quid pro quo arrangement. And MacGregor would be out in the cold.

Four committee members prepped by Eli would support the idea. One of them would suggest they make Herman the recommended candidate. Herman would provide a fresh outlook but was not a stranger. The hospital would be welcoming back one of their own who already had chief experience.

Rose Jackson, the Black woman who represented the medical school, stood to face Eli and began to speak before he gave her permission. "At most of these meetings I have only observed," she said with some passion. "A committee member informed me about the possibility of proposing Dr. Herman for this position. I wish to share some data with you."

Eli sat fuming. *Who on the committee had leaked his plan?*

"While Herman was director of the training program in West Texas, three students of color complained that he discriminated against them and made racist and demeaning comments," Jackson read.

Eli stared at the woman. "Isn't this just hearsay?"

"West Texas University prepared a confidential report," Jackson continued. "I ask that the excerpt I am about to read be entered into our minutes. 'While an important and productive surgeon, Dr. Herman exhibited persistent racial and gender bias. Despite multiple remedial sessions, he maintained that women and people of color could not be good neurosurgeons. The 'cultural limitations' of such people handicapped them in acquiring requisite intellectual and technical skills.'"

Eli realized he would have to do major damage repair for Herman to get the job.

He thanked Jackson as quickly as he could and adjourned the meeting, trying to figure out how he could have her replaced.

He had one path left. He would have a quiet meeting with the hospital president. She was the person with the final say. He could easily undermine Kalangi and Merrek—they were outsiders and the hospital culture did not take kindly to such candidates. Trying to propose Herman might be a little more difficult, but at least he could work to discredit MacGregor to the ultimate decision-maker.

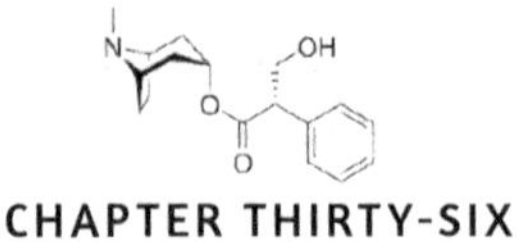

CHAPTER THIRTY-SIX

ELI AND RENWICK

Max Eli entered the office of Dr. Susan Renwick, president of Harbor Hospital, with a simple goal— to convince her that Duncan MacGregor would be a poor choice as Chair of the Department of Neurosurgery. If he could get her to accept Herman as an alternative, so much the better.

He understood that his task was difficult, but he relished the challenge. Renwick was guided by money and prestige. Eli would have to use these to lead her to the conclusion that she should not install MacGregor.

Eli usually felt irritated when he entered the executive suite of the hospital, and today was no exception. Occupying the top floor of the twelve-story building, the complex of rooms was spotless, with a commanding view of the harbor. Much nicer than his fourth-floor Neurology space. The contemporary furniture contributed to the sense of restrained elegance. And the suite always smelled of roses.

Twelve stories below, ferries and pleasure boats dotted the sea, and airplanes took off and landed at Logan Airport across the harbor every two minutes. Eli wondered how

Renwick ever got any work done. In her position, he would sit and watch yachts all day. Hell, if he made the salary she did, he would buy a yacht, not just watch one.

Even before he sat, Eli launched into a long description of the job of a neurosurgery department chair, emphasizing the need for a leader to be present in the hospital at all times. "The fact is that we're having trouble with the neurosurgery chief search," he began, "because MacGregor seems a good candidate, but he's away from the hospital too much of the time. Today we live in such an uncertain world that having a department chief who is away several weeks a year leaves the institution exposed."

"But MacGregor is teaching neurosurgeons in developing countries. That enhances our reputation," Renwick said. "And he has excellent people to cover him when he's away."

"Think of the money lost by his not being able to do surgery during his trips abroad."

"I believe the neurosurgical operating room schedule is full even when MacGregor's not here," Renwick said. "At least the major contribution to our bottom line doesn't dip. His subordinates love it when he's not in town. It gives them a chance to do surgery."

She stood. "I'll tell you what. MacGregor hasn't been around for a couple of days now. Let's go down to the neurosurgery unit and see how it's functioning without him."

As they walked down to the eleventh-floor neurosurgical intensive care unit, she continued, "Have you and Duncan reconciled your differences about intensive care? As I recall, you wanted neurologists to run the neuro ICU and he wanted neurosurgeons. I had to split the baby up—give part to you, part to him. Made me feel a bit like Solomon. How is that working for you?"

"Seems OK," Eli lied. MacGregor had diminished his stature by refusing to let neurologists run the neurosurgical ICU, the practice in many other neurosurgical units. That was one of the reasons he did not want that arrogant Scot as chief.

As they stepped into the unit and put on gowns, hats, and masks, the first striking element was the relative quiet. There were no clanging alarms, calls for code blue, or other emergency events. Despite twenty patients recovering from surgery or neural trauma, the unit was quiet.

"This is a rare treat," the head nurse said as they approached the nursing station. "To what do we owe the honor of a visit from the hospital president and chief of neurology?"

"Just taking a look," Renwick said. "Things slower with MacGregor away?"

"Not at all. He's set the system up to run without him effortlessly. We do miss his smile though. He's a calming presence whenever he's here."

"Thanks," Renwick replied. "Looks like you're busy. We were just passing through."

As they returned to her office, Renwick said, "So international travel doesn't have to diminish work here. It may bring in patients. And it has other benefits. We have just been given some good news about neurosurgery."

Eli felt the pit of his stomach fall. "How so?' His voice was faint, throat suddenly dry.

"A Moroccan businessman named Zadi asked to give ten million dollars to MacGregor personally because of his help with a daughter named Amara."

Eli began to squirm in his chair. "And what happened?"

"Instead of accepting the money for his own use, Mac sent Mr. Zadi to me, and we developed the Zadi professorship in neurosurgery. The money will benefit future generations as well. And it looks like Mr. Zadi's friends are willing to provide further funding for a neuroscience institute."

"That's great news," Eli croaked. "How will the professor be chosen?"

"I trust you will recommend Mac for the job, since that's the only way can get the money. I have no question he is also the most qualified candidate."

"And the director of the neuroscience institute?" Eli could hardly speak.

"Way too early to talk about that. We'll have to see how much our Moroccan connection will provide. I invite you to stay tuned. It's all very exciting for our hospital."

As Eli left the office clenching and unclenching his fists, Renwick called after him. "By the way, MacGregor doesn't know any of this, and I don't think he had any part in arranging it, so I would appreciate it if you kept all this to yourself for now. Nice to see you, Max."

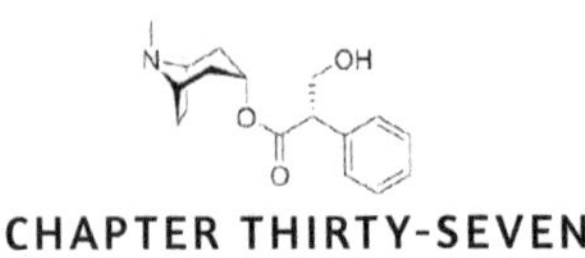

CHAPTER THIRTY-SEVEN

INDEPENDENCE DAY

"It should be fun to have a rooftop table in a building across from the esplanade," Lauren said to Mac as the family squeezed into a trolley in Brookline. "When I was a kid, I always had to watch the ceremonies from the Boston esplanade. It's an unpleasant experience with all those people. Siting on the Cambridge side of the river will make it a lot less crowded. But look around us. Even though it's two hours before the concert, this streetcar is crazy!"

"And will get worse," Mac said, his masked mouth pushed against her ear by the press of passengers. "I used to love the friendly chaos of Boston's July fourth celebration. Now, not so much."

"Will we be able to see the cannons blast during the 1812 overture?" Peter asked.

"Yep," Mac replied.

He gave up trying to talk as new passengers of all ages, color, and lifestyle loaded onto the streetcar. Soon it could not add anyone and left hopefuls standing beside the track as a packed streetcar chain rumbled past. Maggie's shrill voice alerted him minutes later. "Mom, Dad, we're at Park Street. Here's where we change!"

Mac detected a mixed aroma of marijuana and perspiration as the family ploughed through the subterranean crowd to the Red Line connection. The underground Park Street station was stifling

"Do we exit the Red Line at Charles or Kendall?" Maggie asked, waving an MBTA map.

"Kendall," Mac replied. "Our building is on the Cambridge side of the Charles."

They made it safely to the Red Line train, and as they crossed the Longfellow Bridge, saw a flotilla of small boats waiting for the concert and the fireworks. Spectators lounging on blankets lined both sides of the Charles River as far as the eye could see. The two years of cancelled concerts because of COVID seemed to be distant memories. The event was again heading for a million spectators.

Leaving the Red Line at Kendall, they walked back to the banks of the Charles. From the shore they could see the crowd on the Boston side of the river lounging in the July sun on their blankets and lawn chairs. The most enterprising had arrived there at seven a.m., when the esplanade opened. All of them appeared to be enjoying the day, and similar crowds had begun to gather on the Cambridge side of the Charles.

"One thing you don't have to worry about is security in this building," Mac said to Lauren as they approached the Riverside complex. "The people in it are doing very sensitive governmental work. My friend Jim Brogan arranged for us to get in, but it can become a fortress if necessary. No worries about some weirdos passing by and bothering our Independence Day luncheon."

Two security guards checked Mac and the family against a guest list, confirmed their ID, put them through metal detectors, and motioned them to the elevator.

The elevator whisked them up to the rooftop terrace, which was decked out with flags and bunting. Socially distanced tables covered with red, white, and blue tablecloths dotted the floor. About half the seats were already occupied. On the warm July air, the aroma of grilled hamburgers filled the space, reminding Mac of his childhood backyard barbeques.

Shortly after the family arrived at their reserved table, they were disturbed by the noise of the public address system. After crackling, it burst into action with a volume that startled them. "Attention please. This is not a drill. It is necessary to evacuate this building. Attention. This is not a drill. Please evacuate immediately. Attention please…"

The children looked at each other stunned, unsure what to do. Lauren wrapped them in her arms. Mac tried to find someone in authority to address. Diners rose from their seats and moved toward the hallway. Mac and his family followed.

Two security guards, one male and one female, met them at the exit. "I'm sorry, folks," the male guard said. "We have to vacate the building. Follow me to the stairway."

"What's the problem? Fire? Terrorist threat?" Mac and a dozen other people asked.

"Bomb threat next door. Just a precaution to close this building, but we can't take any chances. Another guard will guide you once you get to the sidewalk."

The female guard remained quiet, but something about

her eyes staring above her mask made Mac uneasy. They were dark, merciless eyes. Eyes he had seen somewhere before.

The male guard proceeded to lead the group down the stairs while the PA system continued its deafening message. Loud complaints and a variety of threats issued from the descending group. Despite the panic evident on some faces, the descent was orderly, with new people joining the exodus at each level. The MacGregor children nestled under Lauren's arms, squeezing tightly against her to fit in the stairwell. Mac followed.

As he neared the ground floor, Mac felt a tap on his shoulder. His family continued ahead, but he turned to face the woman guard, who spoke almost directly in his ear. "Dr. MacGregor, we need you to come with me. We have a medical emergency."

Lauren turned back toward them. The guard shouted, "Mrs. MacGregor, we require your husband's assistance." Lauren started to say something but was moved away by the ongoing crowd.

"How did you know my name?" Mac asked. "And what about my family? I belong with them."

"We got your name from the guest list. Your family will be fine."

"What's so important anyway? Aren't there other doctors who can help?" Mac tried to resist and move back toward his disappearing family.

"This is a matter of life and death." The female guard steered him down the stairway toward the basement.

Mac stopped after a few steps. "Where are you taking me? Nobody should be down here."

"You'll see when you get there."

He turned and tried to ascend.

And looked down the barrel of a Glock 17.

"Who are you?" Mac asked, confused and angry. "What's going on?"

"Name's Jane," she said. "Get in there, and I'll tell you what happens next." She pointed to a door marked *Employees Only.*

Once in the room, Jane ordered Mac to sit at a small round table.

"Where's the patient? What's the life and death situation?"

"Your life," Jane hissed. "You have two choices. You can do what I say, and you and your family have a chance of survival, or you can do something stupid, in which case both you and they will die. You'll be the luckier one, though, because your death will be fast. Theirs will not be."

Mac rose and lunged toward her, but her gun butt came down hard on his head as she sidestepped his rush. He fell forward onto the table and felt Jane tether his hands behind his back with plastic ties. Blood dripped onto his face, but he could do nothing about it.

"That counts as stupid, but I'll give you another chance." Jane lowered herself into a seat and examined him as if he were a specimen she had just collected. "I've been waiting to face you for some time, Doctor Duncan MacGregor. You have no tactical military training, but you destroyed a very powerful plan that took a long time to develop. I am going to make you pay for that."

"What plan did I destroy?" Mac's heart began to race.

"Here's what's going to happen," she continued, ignoring his question. "I'm going to give you a chance, rather than killing you outright. I want to see what you're made of. We're both going to drink some special water, then have trial by combat."

"What the hell are you talking about?"

"If you win, you and the family go free because I'll be dead," she continued. "If I win, you all die. That's the way we settled our blood feuds in Sicily." She slammed her fist down on the table. "Damn, I've been so looking forward to this. I'm going to make sure we have at least two hours before the place is cleared. We white folks are going to take back this country. and it's going to start here."

She took a pouch from her pocket, poured water into two glasses, and tapped powder from the pouch into each glass. "In case you think I'm giving you something different from me, I'll switch the glasses several times."

Mac sat dumbfounded, trying to comprehend what insanity he had joined.

"Open wide, Doctor," Jane said.

Mac clamped his mouth shut.

Jane squeezed his nostrils closed with her left hand. He tried to twist his head and dislodge her, but she kept firm pressure. He could not breathe with his mouth and nose closed off. She stood staring at him with those merciless eyes, waiting for his breath-holding to fail.

The moment he opened his mouth and gulped in air, she poured half the contents of the glass down his throat and held his jaw tightly closed. He sputtered and coughed but had to swallow the liquid. A little spilled onto his shirt. He clamped his mouth shut again, but the moment he had to breathe again, she emptied the rest of the glass into his gullet.

Jane emptied her glass of liquid in one gulp, then checked her watch. "I have to go upstairs to initiate lockout mode—no one will be able to enter for two hours. I can just imagine your family frantic at the door. And all those VIP's who don't get their barbecue." She tied his arms and legs with zip-ties and stuffed a rag into his throat. "Not that anyone would hear your shouts anyway. Don't go anywhere! I'll be back."

She disappeared through the doorway.

Left alone, Mac felt his stomach sink as he tried to understand what was going on. Of course, this was Jane of the *Sakinah,* who somehow escaped the slaughter on the ship. There was little chance he could best her in hand-to-hand combat, even enhanced by whatever powers the powder bestowed.

He had to get away from this room.

He hauled himself to a standing position and looked around. What could he use to cut the wrist bands? He gazed at the lockers with their posters, the metal desk of the superintendent, the microwave, the refrigerator.

A letter opener on the desk. No sharp edge at all.

Scissors. He couldn't use them with his hands tied.

He hobbled over to the closed locker and worked the door open. A shaving kit hung from it. He moved the kit to the desk and found a razor, an old-fashioned two-edged Western model. Opening the carrier, he removed the blade. He could manipulate it now to saw against the first zip tie.

Agonizing, slow, painful, but one by one the bands were severed. He was sweating after a few minutes, perspiring with focused exertion and anxiety that he would not get done in time. Several small lacerations bled over his hands.

As the ties divided, he had more room to work the blade. He cut the last strands quicker than the first, and his wrists were free.

His task was complicated by an increasing feeling that he should just push the damned ties against the blade and forget about being so careful. Chances are he would be fine, and even if he had a small cut, that would be easy to deal with. Why be so tentative? He could handle this and anything else, including the bitch Jane.

He sawed through his leg bands. He was free.

Striding toward the door, he ripped the rag from his mouth.

And looked up to see Jane filling the doorway.

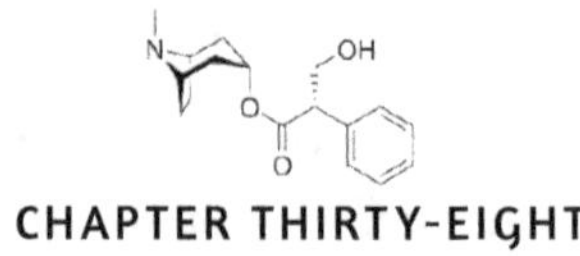

CHAPTER THIRTY-EIGHT

BERSERKER SMACKDOWN

Jane blocked the door, eyes blazing with triumphant energy. "The building will stay in lockout mode for two hours," she said. "All internal doors are open, but no one can enter or exit. And nobody can change the parameters. They're built in as a defense for this super-secure fortress."

She moved closer and almost spit out the words. "I've waited a long time for this, MacGregor. I want the pleasure of hunting you down, of seeing you sweat before you die. You're not just another kill for me. You're the reason my whole plan failed."

"Your plan?" Mac croaked, desperately trying to buy time.

"To restore this country to the white people who created it. Get rid of the Blacks and Hispanics and Asians and all those who are dragging it down today." She looked at her watch. "I'm a good sport. I'll give you a five-minute head start. After that, I'll track you down and kill you."

"What are you talking about?" Mac said. "This is Cambridge Massachusetts. You can't just…"

"The countdown has started," Jane said, tapping her wrist.

Run, Mac thought. *Just run. It's your only chance.*

He raced into the corridor like a hunted animal, trying to formulate a plan. The woman had changed a pleasant family outing into a desperate fight for his life. There was no question in his mind that after assassinating him, she would kill his wife and children. He would have to defeat her now and forever.

He paused as he ran past the building directory, looking for rooms that would allow a hiding place and provide something useful as a weapon.

Offices would be no help, especially the open offices of this company. Bathrooms would also be useless. They were traps that would give him no hiding place.

Two locations might provide the combination of hiding and weaponry he needed: the daycare center on this level, and the gym two floors above. If those failed, there was always the terrace he had started dinner on earlier that night. That might provide a path of escape.

He found and entered the daycare facility, locked the door, and flicked on the lights. Twenty by forty feet, all windows shuttered by the lockdown. Teachers' desks at the front, with small chairs arranged in a semicircle. Cubbies for jackets and lunch boxes and nap blankets, storage containers filled with miniature cars and Legos, inspirational posters and picture of the children and teachers on the wall.

He emptied the tub of wheelie cars and Legos on the floor in front of the door, so Jane would find her footing precarious if she entered the room.

Anger built within him, along with a conviction he could take this woman in one-on-one combat. What right did she have to threaten him and his family? He was strong and smart, and he had everything to fight for. She was nothing.

A sense of invincibility infused his body and mind. He could feel the spirit of his ancestor Bhaltair MacGregor replacing Duncan MacGregor's civilized soul. Bhaltair had slaughtered thirty Englishmen single-handedly at the battle of Culloden. Why should Duncan hesitate about attacking one woman?

He had to restrain himself from opening the door and running down the hallway to confront Jane right now. He looked at his watch. Four minutes had passed. Although he knew he had to think about an overall plan, he could come up with nothing except the idea of attacking with direct overwhelming force. Bhaltair was winning.

Which, Duncan said within him, *would be fatal. In direct battle without subterfuge or surprise, I would stand no chance against Jane, the trained soldier who faced me.*

He picked up a small wooden chair, turned off the lights, and took a position beside the doorway. He would knock Jane out as she entered the dark room. If she didn't go down with his blow, she would slip and slide on the toys when she continued into the room and flounder on the floor. An injured fly to be swatted.

He tried to formulate a further plan if that failed, but his mind could not focus. It was filled only with the hatred he had for this woman and how he would avenge the threat she had created. There was no room for reason.

He heard footsteps in the corridor and then a childish voice calling, "Ready or not, here I come." Jane seemed to consider this a game. *How had she guessed so fast he would be in the day care center?*

The door splintered open and fell to the floor, torn off its hinges by a powerful kick. Light from the corridor streamed into the room and Jane, standing on the flattened door, peered into the darkness.

Mac swung the chair, using both arms and body to create maximum momentum.

Even with a surprise attack, Jane had a sixth sense. She ducked before impact and the chair slid across the top of her scalp. She shook her head and made a beeline to Mac.

He backed away, stepping onto the wheelie cars he had spread on the floor. He felt his feet go out from under him, desperately flung his arms out, tried to regain his balance, and fell onto the floor on his back.

Jane almost stumbled over his supine body as she rocketed toward him. She leapt off the flattened door that had provided a safe surface for her to maneuver, tottered on the wheelie cars, cursed, and slammed to the floor as well.

Mac rolled over and over, enduring the pain of multiple Legos and matchbox cars digging into him until he reached the flattened door. He scrambled onto its smooth surface and ran for the corridor.

If he ever needed a reminder that a one-on-one confrontation would be disastrous, he had just received one.

He ran up the stairs two at a time to the gym floor. Entering the exercise room, he passed the rowing machines, treadmills, and ellipticals, following signs to the sauna.

A manikin outside the trainer's office displayed the male body with its muscle groups. Mac grabbed it and the thick metal rod that suspended it, dragged both into the sauna. Twisting the thermostat as high as possible, he pushed the temperature into the red zone.

The danger plaque on the wall warned that this temperature could be tolerated for a maximum of five minutes.

The door of the sauna had a small glass window and a wooden handle shaped like a sideways U. Yanking the door open, Mac sat the naked manikin on the far corner of the wooden shelf and placed a towel over its groin. With the wooden ladle and bucket provided, he poured water on coals that were now red hot, sizzling with each drop of water, producing steam so dense he could barely breathe.

He gulped in fresh air as he exited and retrieved the rod that had held the mannikin. If Jane entered the sauna to attack the decoy, he would jam the rod into the space formed by the handle on the door and its twin on the frame. That would lock her in. Not even a trained warrior could tolerate that heat for long. She would boil and die.

Mac took a position behind a shower curtain in the room beside the sauna and waited. Bhaltair grew stronger within him each minute, shouting that he could vanquish any woman. Wouldn't it be best for him to confront her directly in one glorious battle? That part of Duncan MacGregor felt empowered, revved up, fully alert and ready to kick ass.

Somewhere deep in his mind, Mac's voice whispered, *this is the powder talking. If you confront Jane, you're done for. Keep to the plan. Avoid her.*

Footsteps interrupted his internal dialogue. They stopped at several points in the exercise room, then approached the sauna. Mac peered around the curtain, saw Jane stare through the small glass window in the sauna door, pull the door open, and disappear.

He raced from his post and rammed the metal rod to lock the two door handles. Jane was now trapped in a space whose temperature was above one hundred thirty degrees. With luck, she would succumb in short order.

Howls filled the gym. Mac imagined her realizing the trap, trying to escape from the brutal heat, and feeling the scorching steam burn her lungs and skin.

The sound of fracturing glass interrupted his imaginings. He saw a boot held by a blistered arm smash through the broken window in the sauna door. Lacerations from the glass shards bled as the arm felt for the rod and began to move it out of its locking position. Within a few seconds the door burst open and Jane stood defiant, face and limbs reddened and blistered, eyes wild, hair matted.

"So now you face her and finish her off," Bhaltair MacGregor shouted within Mac. *"You've got the advantage, Laddie. Use it!"*

Duncan within him argued for moderation.

MacGregor decided the best course was to fall back. In the battle, a blow to Jane's head and boiling in the sauna had failed. He had no idea what he should try next.

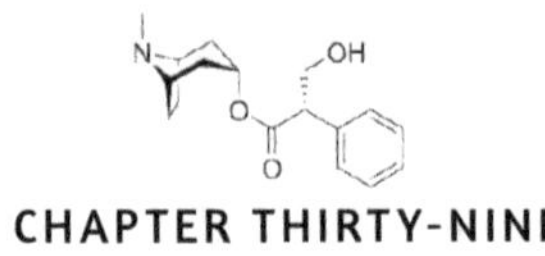

CHAPTER THIRTY-NINE

FIGHT TO THE DEATH

CAMBRIDGE, MA
JULY 4, 2021

From the shower stall, Mac watched Jane scan the room, peeling away clothing and skin from her blistered body. She did not grimace, despite what must have been intense pain.

He backed away from the shower curtain to remain hidden as her head swiveled toward his position. His palms dripped with sweat, and he held his breath. *How had she managed to survive steaming heat that long?* When he looked again, he saw her moving away from him.

Mac sprinted in the opposite direction, heading toward exit signs that led to a rear staircase. He ascended as fast as he could, hoping he could reach the terrace and signal for help before Jane could follow.

The staircase ended in glass doors with darkness beyond them. Mac entered and flicked on the wall switch. Lights blazed to illuminate the area as though it were mid-day. He stood in the terrace that had started his evening, now shuttered as part of the lockdown.

Evidence of hasty desertion littered the room festively laid out only two hours before. Abandoned tables with chairs knocked over, half-eaten hamburgers and hot dogs, and open champagne bottles with corks beside them, marked the end of happy family gatherings. Only the flagstaffs at one end of the room remained intact, their sharply pointed metal tips shining in the fluorescent light.

Metal shutters sealed the entire space. Mac realized that there would be no communication with the outside world from here. He moved toward the flag stand, away from the glass door that provided the only access to the room. He still felt rage, believed in his heart he could deal with the woman who was still tracking him. She had just been lucky thus far.

Shattering glass erupted from the doorway he had just left behind. Swiveling, Mac felt his head pound as Jane appeared through the shards of the entry door. She tossed aside the chair that smashed the glass and stepped into the room.

She seemed unsteady, staggering and shaking her head. Mac yanked an American flag from its stand and deployed the staff like a pike, racing toward her. The stars and stripes quivered as he charged.

Jane fixed him with blazing eyes through a face distorted and swollen from the sauna steam. With a loud roar, she stepped aside, yanked the flagpole from his grip, lifted one foot to a chair, and broke the pole in half over her knee. With a smooth continuous motion, she hurtled the sharp tip at Mac's head as he hurtled past.

Mac twisted to avoid the projectile, but the move left him unsteady on his feet. Before he could regain his balance, Jane raced toward him and kicked his legs from under him.

He landed on his back. She pounced on top of him, clutching his shoulders with both hands and butting his face with her forehead.

He was trapped under her body. She hit his face again and again with her forehead, fracturing his nose with a loud crack. Blood dripped down his chin. Intense pain shot through his face and warm liquid trickled into his throat.

If this continues, I'm going to die. Jane had him completely constrained. With knees on his chest and his torso gripped between her legs, she lifted her head higher and higher with each blow, bringing his mid-face closer to caving in.

Mac reached blindly along the floor to find anything that might help, felt the sharp tip of the flagpole. He could see Jane's blistered face, exposed nose cartilage, dark bloodshot eyes, could smell her foul breath as she lifted her head to begin the final blows.

He grabbed the flagpole tip and swung it to meet her forehead as she rocketed toward him. The metal point entered her right eye with such impact that the eye socket exploded with an ear-splitting crunch. The eyeball blew out of the socket and fragments of Jane's brain spilled over him, accompanied by blood and spinal fluid.

Jane clasped her head with both blistered hands and screamed, climbing off him.

She's done for, Mac thought.

He waited for her to collapse.

Instead, she shook her head, spraying red liquid from her

eye socket like a dog shaking off water, and seemed to gain a second wind.

What the hell is going on? How could a ruptured eyeball and smashed eye socket make someone better?

Brain hemorrhage that had suddenly been decompressed. Her amygdala had bled, but the opening in the eye relieved the pressure of the clot building up inside the skull.

Jane stepped back, circling like a huge bird about to finish its prey. She now appeared focused, steady, brandishing the fragment of flagpole that had pierced her own skull and taunting Mac with it. She said nothing, just glared with a one-eyed stare.

Mac palmed a champagne cork from the nearest table. His only hope was to plug the opening created by the destruction of the bony eye socket and let the brain pressure increase again.

Jane charged. Mac tripped her as she rocketed past him, then jumped on her back as she fell. With his right hand, he pounded the cork into her right eye socket to seal it.

Jane writhed to dislodge him. Instead of resisting her, he jumped to his feet and ran to the nearest table.

She flipped to her feet and raced toward him, brandishing the sharp flagpole fragment above her head like a lance. Mac pushed one table after another in her path as she tried to catch him.

Around and around they went, partners in a bizarre dance of death.

Suddenly, Mac realized she had maneuvered him into a corner from which he could not escape. She drew back with the sharp flagpole tip in both hands, raised it above her head to deliver the final blow, staggered toward him, took a deep breath—

And collapsed.

Mac stared at the unmoving body in front of him, felt for a pulse and realized there was none. Jane was dead, killed by the pressure of a brain hemorrhage inside a rigid skull. Both heart and breathing had stopped because of the brain pressure that had built up once he sealed the leak.

He slumped against a wall and closed his eyes.

The sounds of scraping metal alerted him. He watched dazed as the shutters of the terrace opened, letting in the rays of the setting sun. A flood of police in protective gear poured through the doorway. At their head was Brogan, who raced toward him.

"You OK, Mac? What the hell happened?" Brogan asked, his face lined with concern.

"I'll tell you all about it after I see my family."

"You're in no condition to see anyone."

An officer tapped Brogan on the shoulder. "Chief, that woman's dead," he said, pointing toward Jane.

"I want to see my family. Now." Mac pulled himself to his feet and staggered toward the door.

Brogan put an arm around him and cleared the way through the swarm of police. "I don't know how you did it, but you just took out one of the deadliest domestic terrorist we've ever had to deal with."

"I need to see Lauren and the kids," Mac shouted. "Where are they?"

"We've tried to make them comfortable at the hotel down the street. They've been waiting for you to come back when the shutters of the building open. We told them you were locked in by the system but were otherwise OK."

"Do they know about Jane?"

"No."

"When can I be with them?" Mac asked.

"I have a car waiting downstairs, but there's no way you can see them in your present condition. You look terrible."

Mac put a hand to his face, looked at his fingers tinged with blood.

"You need to take a couple of minutes to wash up. And here, put on this shirt and jacket. I keep it in my vehicle in case of emergencies."

He handed Mac a blue shirt with a button-down collar, then steered him into the men's room and stood guard outside. Facing the mirror, Mac hardly recognized his own bruised and battered face. He washed away the blood where he could and tried to remove the red stains from his shirt and jacket.

He gave up, threw both jacket and shirt in the trash, and put on Brogan's garments, which fit reasonably well. He could feel his eyes swelling and could hardly breathe through his nose, but at least the blood was gone.

With exhaustion fast overtaking him, Mac moved to the street from the elevator. The July fourth crowd packed the sidewalk now that the emergency was over, and Brogan had to support him as they ducked into the waiting limousine. Once they had pulled away, Mac asked, "Was there really a bomb?"

"Yes," Brogan replied. "It took our EOD squad to find it. And it was active, the kind of device used by our own troops in Afghanistan."

"So it was Jane all the way?"

"I think so. I expect she planted it earlier today, then 'found' it as she was inspecting the building. The alarm that followed allowed her to initiate the emergency lockdown protocol."

"And there was no way to open the building?"

"Correct. No one could get in for two hours with the lockout parameters she set."

Mac lay his head back until they finished the short trip to the hotel.

"We're here," Brogan said, escorting Mac to the door of the family's room. "I'll leave now, but when you're finished, we'll do a quick debrief. Thank you for all you've done. Uncovering this plot and dispatching Jane helped save us. It's too bad no one will ever know."

Maggie and Peter ran to hug their father as soon as he opened the door. They stopped as they got closer.

"Daddy, what happened to you?" Maggie asked. "Your face is all scratched up and puffy."

"I'm sorry, pumpkin. I ran into some nasty people." Mac said.

"Was there an explosion?" Peter asked. "How come we didn't hear it? What happened to the bomb? Did they disarm it?"

They both put arms around him. Lauren lagged a few steps in joining the group embrace, but squeezed as hard as the children after the first moments.

With the embrace finished, she stood back. "That's a very nice shirt and jacket you're wearing," she said. "I don't remember one quite like it in your wardrobe."

Mac had no answers. He just stared at Lauren, so grateful he was able to be with her again.

"We were worried about you," Maggie said, "but the lady guard explained you were helping somebody. Are they OK?"

"Sort of," Mac said.

"It was so cool to see the EOD squad take the bomb away," Peter said. "Better than fireworks any day."

"What's the EOD squad?" Maggie asked.

"Explosive Ordinance Device," Peter said with a superior look. "Don't you know? They're the specialists that deal with bombs and stuff."

"Once they told us the bomb was gone, we knew you'd be fine," Maggie said. "I just wish they could have opened the building so we could see you sooner. It was really weird to watch it close down with all those metal shutters. Like a fort."

"Dad, we have the best times when we do something special with you," Peter said.

Lauren said nothing, but she did smile through her tears, and that was all Mac wanted to see.

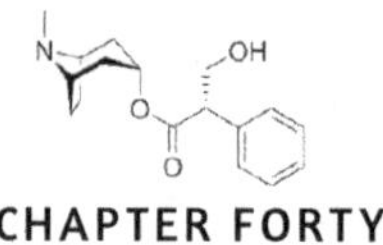

CHAPTER FORTY

POST-MORTEM

Two weeks after Jane died, Mac invited Brogan to watch the cutting of her brain, He explained to Brogan that the time interval was necessary to let fixative solution solidify her brain tissue and that the autopsy would tell precisely what killed her.

Brogan did not seem eager to participate at first, but ultimately agreed to accompany Mac.

They met in the sixth-floor cafeteria terrace of Harbor Hospital shortly before the brain cutting. Downing cups of strong coffee, they watched planes take off and arrive at Logan and boats scurry back and forth in the ocean below them. Mac commented that he had come close to never seeing this scene again. "Can you imagine what would have happened if Jane had succeeded?" he asked.

"I try not to think about that," Brogan said.

"What's next for you?" Mac asked.

"I've been recalled to Langley."

"Bad or good?" Mac asked.

"Good. The agency likes what we did, even though it will not be public knowledge any time soon. They've promoted me to section chief for Terrorism Analysis, a job I've always wanted."

"Congratulations!"

"The new position allows me to oversee worldwide surveillance and also work in the field. But how about you? Any news on the chief position at the hospital yet?"

"Still no final word," Mac said, looking at his watch. "We should get downstairs to see Dr. Wu at work." They left the cafeteria and while they waited for the elevator. Mac continued his conversation. "My friends tell me the only thing worse than being chief is not being chief. Administration is not my skill, and being chief has a lot of that."

"You get used to the bureaucracy," Brogan said. "Sometimes it can even be useful."

"One thing has happened that will definitely help," Mac said. "Amara Zadi's father has created a hospital fund to support my salary. I can spend my time on what I love whether I become chief or not. I'm just sorry Amara felt she had to leave Tangier. Being away will be hard on her dad."

"Lyon is a great city, and her new job with Interpol should let her flourish. The Tangier police are still sorting themselves out. It's hard to identify all the rotten apples in that barrel, and she's smart to be out of it."

Mac thought Brogan looked anxious as they approached the autopsy room. "You don't have to watch this, you know," Mac said.

"I'll be OK. I do want to see what made Jane stop ticking."

As they entered the autopsy room, the acrid odor of fixative made Mac wince despite his splinted and packed nose.

Brogan stepped back, shook his head, and added a second mask, saying "On second thought, I think I'll just watch from the bleachers."

Dr. Wu was waiting for them. As they entered, she gowned, gloved, masked, and perched on a stool in front of a stainless-steel table. A grey brain about the size of a cabbage sat in a dish in front of her. "Welcome," she said as the men entered. "Ready to start?"

Mac nodded.

Using a long blunt-tipped knife, Grace sliced through the front third of the brain with one definitive cut. She held the fragment she had just separated to display a large purple mass that looked like grape jelly deep in the right half of the cerebral hemisphere. "Here's what killed Jane Russo," she said, "a massive brain hemorrhage that started in the amygdala." She stared at Mac. "The clot was the cause of death."

"What about the orbital fracture and the cork?" Mac asked.

"The orbital blowout decompressed the brain temporarily to restore normal pressure, and the impacted champagne cork returned the pressure to fatal levels. You can see the signs of brain stem pressure here." Grace pointed to notches in the brain stem from compression against rigid structures in the skull, "Death would have happened in a few minutes anyway. The cork just hastened the process."

"I didn't have a few minutes," Mac muttered, heart racing as he remembered the frantic events of July fourth.

"Fate had already killed her," Grace said. "That's why

I'm signing out the cause of death as a massive brain hemorrhage, period."

"So with the escape route through the eye socket blocked, the pressure inside the head built up, her breathing stopped, and she died?" Brogan said. "Seems so mechanical."

"But that's precisely what happened," Grace said.

"And the genetic studies?" Mac asked.

"Jane lacked the gene to metabolize the Berserker drug. That's why her amygdala blew out."

"But my impression was that she thought she was in the white superclass," Brogan said.

"This is not my field," Grace said, "but my experience as an Asian has made me sensitive to the issue. Most white supremacists make the same mistake of thinking they are purebloods." Wu replied. "They don't understand genetics. Most of us have a mixture of genes. A sense of entitlement, not genes, make these people think they are superior. Jane just wasn't as Aryan as she thought she was. She was mixed race, as most of us are."

Brogan interrupted. "I don't know about genes, Mac, but if I had any idea that asking you to look into a hyper-violent monkey six months ago would have led to this, I would have thought twice about my request."

"Maybe you should have thought more than twice," Mac said.

"In the end, it worked out well," Brogan said. "We disabled a domestic terrorist network and seized a compound that could have cost millions of American lives."

"And almost got killed in the process," Mac said. "I need

a change. My next travels are going to be with the family for pleasure."

"Any thoughts where?" Brogan asked.

"Wherever my wife wants to go. I'm going to focus on her and the children for a while. At the moment, she's talking about a vacation in Istanbul."

THE END

AUTHOR'S NOTE

This story is intended as fiction although it does describe actual events during the siege of the United States Capitol by domestic terrorists on January 6, 2021.

The idea of henbane as an agent promoting violence is at least as old as the ancient Greeks. Its properties of anesthesia, visual distortion and disinhibition made it a potent facilitator to aggressive behavior. Recently, the suggestion has surfaced that henbane made the Viking Berserkers berserk.[1]

I am not aware of a gene that allows henbane to be metabolized more quickly in one ethnic group versus another, but we know alcohol and other drugs have genetic differences in metabolism.

As ever, I am grateful to Carole Holladay for her advice and support for this book. My reading group—Hans and Judy Copek, Shelly Karol, Cheryl Lawton-Malone, Carol Lynn, and Sean Harding—were most helpful during the development of the story.

Mike Abram, Sal Tripple, Christopher Black, Dorian Mintzer, and Alex Malozemoff acted as beta readers and gave valuable suggestions.

Mayapriya Long of Bookwrights and the crew at Skean Dhu Press did their usual magic to bring the book into being.

I am grateful to these and other colleagues for helping with the book. Most of all, however, I am grateful to those law officers and others who risk their lives every day in the attempt to stop the wave of domestic terrorism that seems to be washing over our country.

Boston, MA
July 2022

1. Fatur, K. "Sagas of the Solanaceae: Speculative ethnobotanical perspective on the Norse berserkers." *Journal of Ethnoparmacology* 244:112-151, 15 November 2019

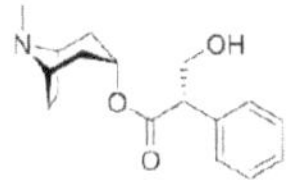

THE AUTHOR

Dr. Peter Black has been a physician to Congress and the Supreme Court, professor of neurosurgery at Harvard Medical School, and President of the World Federation of Neurosurgical Societies.

Berserkers is the third book in his Duncan MacGregor thriller series. *Seizure*, the first in the series, won the *Writer's Digest* prize for best indie genre fiction of 2021. Genre fiction includes mysteries, thrillers, westerns, and romance.

Dr. Black divides his time between Boston and London. He can be found on the web at peterblackbooks.com, on Facebook as peterblackbooks, and on Twitter as @peterblackbooks2. His books are available on Amazon.com.